Transmission along
the Meridian
MERIDIAN QIGONG

Compiled and Presented by: Li Ding

FOREIGN LANGUAGES PRESS BEIJING

First Edition 1988
Second Printing 1993

Translated by Li Dong and Hou Min
Copy edited by Anne Stevenson

ISBN 0-8351-2322-7
ISBN 7-119-00777-7

© Foreign Languages Press, Beijing, 1988

Published by Foreign Languages Press
24 Baiwanzhuang Road, Beijing 100037, China

Printed by Beijing Foreign Languages Printing House
19 Chegongzhuang Xilu, Beijing 100044, China
Printed in the People's Republic of China

ABOUT THE AUTHOR

Professor Li Ding was born in Henan Province, China in 1935. He graduated from Shanxi Medical College (China) in 1960. He is now a member of the Board of Directors of the All-China Association of Acupuncture and Moxibustion, vice-director and vice-secretary general of the Shanxi Society of Acupuncture and Moxibustion, executive member of the Board of Directors of the Taiyuan Society of Acupuncture and Moxibustion, and president of the Qigong Society of Shanxi Medical College. With traditional Chinese medicine as the main approach, he combines traditional Chinese and Western medicine in disease treatment and prevention. Over the last twenty-seven years, he has published more than ten books on acupuncture, traditional Chinese medicine, and Chinese pharmacology, including *Jianmei Jinlou Tu* and *A Collection of TCM Clinical Experience*. He was invited to give lectures on acupuncture and Chinese Qigong in Italy in 1987.

MERIDIAN QIGONG

The author, Professor Li Ding, a prominent TCM (traditional Chinese medicine) doctor and acupuncturist, is a strong supporter of Qigong for maintaining health. The theories of the Zang-fu (internal organs) and meridians from traditional Chinese Qigong are the theoretical basis of this process designed to regulate the brain's functioning, the respiration and the strength. On this theoretical basis the book *Meridian Qigong* rests. Following step by step the book's explanations and with twenty minutes' practice, anyone can learn a bit about the relationships of the organs, among the flow routes of the fourteen meridians and the connections of the meridians with the nine orifices (eyes, ears, nostrils, mouth, urethra and anus) and 316 acupuncture points.

This kind of Qigong is fairly recent. Since November 1985, the Shanxi TV Station has reported on this new Qigong, and an introduction to it has appeared in installments in the magazine *Scientific Friends*. Professor Li Ding has written this book, *Meridian Qigong*, to respond to requests from viewers and readers who expressed intense interest in this kind of Qigong, which is so effective against difficult and chronic diseases.

The book has three chapters and fourteen sections. It includes 238 photos and 14 plates showing the meridians. The book is also complete with a video tape

(30 minutes) to make it easier for practitioners to study, practice and master this Qigong.

Meridian Qigong also can be a useful reference for scientific research personnel and medical workers doing scientific research, teaching and clinical treatment utilizing Qigong. So this volume is useful for instruction and reference alike.

FOREWORD

Qigong is a Chinese discipline used for the protection of health, and it has a history spanning 3,000 years. It has been shown to have particularly outstanding effects in treating chronic and difficult diseases. Generally speaking, Qigong is divided into two types. One is the quiescent type, which is meant to be performed standing, sitting, or lying down using special breathing techniques by which the practitioner learns to focus his mind. The other one is the mobile type, which employs lithe movements and massage while keeping a proper balance between mind and emotion, Qi and strength. Internally, Qigong can enhance the spirit, the Qi and the mind. Externally, it can strengthen the tendons, bones and skin. Therefore, Qigong exercise can regulate the functioning of the brain, promote the functioning of the circulatory, digestive and other systems, and bring the latent power of cells into play. For optimal results, one should practice Qigong assiduously and with perseverance, and the body will be strengthened and resistance against disease increased; some illnesses will be cured, and life may be prolonged.

Meridian Qigong is the Qigong which combines motion with quiescence. It comes from scientifically and organically combining the theories of the Zang-fu and meridians with traditional Qigong's theory of transmitting Qi and regulating respiration. Since

Meridian Qigong came to the forefront in 1985, it has been well received. People have come from Singapore, India, Germany, the USA, the UK, Belgium, and Norway to study it. This Meridian Qigong has been along the meridians.

This Qigong uses the 12 standard meridians and the Ren and Du meridians. Thus Qigong has also been called "the 14 meridians Qigong." I have tried to show in detail with drawings the flow routes and the connections of the meridians. For each of the meridians I have explained the flow routes and indications and have given step-by-step instructions. What in the past has been translated into English as "channel" has most recently been approved to be termed "meridian," and that is the terminology I have employed throughout this book.

I am aware that there are shortcomings in this book. However, in the short time we had in which to prepare the manuscript for publication, we have done our best. Nevertheless, any suggestions or criticisms will be appreciated for future revision.

Professor Li Ding, July 1987

CONTENTS

CHAPTER 1 THE GENERAL CONCEPTS OF MERIDIAN QIGONG   1
  I. Introduction   1
  II. Preserving General Resistance: Correspondences Between Man and Nature   2
  III. Regulation of Mind, Respiration and Energy   5
    A. Regulation of Mind: Circulation of Qi Along the Meridians Stabilizing the Seven Emotions   5
    B. Inhaling and Exhaling: Regulation of Respiration Storage of Energy and Accumulation of Oxygen   6
    C. Motion and Stillness: Activation of the Limbs by Massage to Regulate Energy   7
  IV. How to Practice   8
  V. Notes on Practicing Meridian Qigong   8
    A. Requirements Before Practicing   8
    B. Requirements During the Practice   10
    C. Requirements for Ending the Practice   10
    D. Effects of Practice   10
  VI. Tailoring Meridian Qigong Practice to Particular Disorders   11

CHAPTER 2 STARTING FORM   14
  I. Put Qi into Dantian   14
  II. Exhalation and Inhalation   20

CHAPTER 3 THE 14 MERIDIANS — 25

- I. The Lung Meridian of the Hand-Taiyin — 25
- II. The Large Intestine Meridian of the Hand-Yangming — 41
- III. The Stomach Meridian of the Foot-Yangming — 59
- IV. The Spleen Meridian of the Foot-Taiyin — 79
- V. The Heart Meridian of the Hand-Shaoyin — 95
- VI. The Small Intestine Meridian of the Hand-Taiyang — 111
- VII. The Bladder Meridian of the Foot-Taiyang — 127
- VIII. The Kidney Meridian of the Foot-Shaoyin — 147
- IX. The Pericardium Meridian of the Hand-Jueyin — 163
- X. The Sanjiao Meridian of the Hand-Shaoyang — 179
- XI. The Gall Bladder Meridian of the Foot-Shaoyang — 195
- XII. The Liver Meridian of the Foot-Jueyin — 217
- XIII. The Ren Meridian — 235
- XIV. The Du Meridian — 247

CHAPTER 1

THE GENERAL CONCEPTS OF MERIDIAN QIGONG

I. Introduction

Qigong, also called "Dao Yin" and "Tu Na," has a history of more than 3,000 years. It is one of the legacies in the treasure-house of traditional Chinese medicine. Though old, it remains even today a very popular subject. The practice of Qigong causes one to exhale waste Qi, inhale fresh Qi, preserve anti-pathogenic Qi in the body, strengthen the health, resist senility, and prolong life. The actual practice of Qigong began in the fourth century A.D. Since then a great number of people have benefited from it. When practiced for a period of time, one can become aware of a stream of heat (vital energy) or Qi being transmitted through the body. Sometimes this can be released from the body, and then it is known as external Qi. Internal Qi, on the other hand, follows the meridians and collaterals within the body; the meridian theory of acupuncture is the keystone of Meridian Qigong. It is the meridian and collateral systems that link the five viscera and six entrails, limbs and bones, five senses and nine orifices with the various tissues and organs of the superficial portion of the body, giving the body organic integrity. The systems of meridians and collaterals are quite complex. The meridian system consists of the regular meridians and extra meridians, whereas the collateral system is composed of the Bie collaterals, Sun collaterals and Fu collaterals. Additionally, there are 36 other meridians including 12 tendon meridians and 12 skin meridians. However, the main trunks are the 12 regular meridians and the Du and Ren Meridians.

In Meridian Qigong, the Qi is transmitted along the 14 meridians and connections while respiration is regulated and movements are controlled. If one practices Meridian Qigong moving from one meridian to another with persistence, the internal Qi will move through the meridians, blocks within the meridians and collaterals will be removed, the Qi and blood will synergize, and the anti-pathogenic Qi will be preserved within the body. People in poor health will strengthen their bodies; patients will eliminate diseases; the elderly will prolong their lives. Meridian Qigong, created on the basis of traditional Chinese medical Qigong, is a mobile yet still, strong yet a gentle exercise which connects organically the Zang-fu and meridian theories with Qigong's circulation of Qi and regulation of respiration.

II. Preserving General Resistance: Correspondences Between Man and Nature

Man lives in nature and has a close relationship with

it. Various changes in nature, such as those related to weather and geographic conditions, directly influence human physiology in development, growth, senility, and disease. In other words, changes in nature are reflected in internal changes of the body; however, at the same time, man has learned to adapt to these natural changes and, also, has learned actively to change nature. This process is known as the correspondence between man and nature.

In the course of a year, there are four primary weather changes. Spring is warm; summer is hot; autumn is cool; winter is cold. So man adapts to such changing conditions through the regulation of body functions, including of Qi and blood. During spring and summer, Yang or "positive" Qi is released, and Qi and blood tend to circulate superficially, so the skin is looser and produces a lot of sweat; whereas during autumn and winter, Yang Qi is stored and Qi and blood tend to circulate more internally, so the skin is tight and produces less sweat, more urine. But when there are abnormal changes in the weather that are beyond the adaptive capacities of the body, dysfunctions of the body may result. The same holds true with the response of the body to changes in the geographic environment. Each individual has different adaptive abilities, so the response to the same environment differs among individuals. Therefore, those who do not adapt will most probably suffer from diseases.

Then how can one promote and strengthen the regulative adaptability to changes in the natural environment so as to resist disease? As a result of their long struggle with nature and against disease, the ancient Chinese working people developed an efficient skill called Qigong for strengthening the internal regulation of the body. It focuses the mind, regulates the respiration and exercises the limbs through the active use of a stream of consciousness. Anti-pathogenic Qi is thus preserved in the body, evil elements blocked, correspondence maintained between man and nature, and the body enabled to adapt to changes in the natural environment. These are the effects of modern Qigong. In fact, Qigong has been found to be especially beneficial when used against chronic and difficult diseases, because it develops the regulative ability of the body, promotes immunological functions, and accelerates recovery.

The occurrence or invasion, change or prognosis of some diseases is the struggle between the anti-pathogenic Qi factor and the pathogenic Qi factor and depends on the balance between the two. When anti-pathogenic Qi predominates over pathogenic Qi, diseases are cured, whereas, when anti-pathogenic Qi is consumed and pathogenic Qi is out of control, the disease becomes more serious and can even cause death. So anti-pathogenic Qi is the root and sustainer of life.

Anti-pathogenic Qi is the ability of the body to resist various pathogenic factors in the environment, to keep a relative balance between Yin and Yang, and to adapt to inside and outside changes the body. These abilities depend on the normal functioning of Zang-fu and sufficient levels of the essences Qi and spirit.

Pathogenic Qi refers to various factors that cause confusion of the Zang-fu's functions, such as wind, cold, summer heat, dampness, dryness, and unnatural heat (fire, wild heat) and changes in the weather.

III. Regulation of Mind, Respiration and Energy

A. Regulation of Mind: Circulation of Qi Along the Meridians Stabilizing the Seven Emotions

In traditional Chinese medicine, man's mental activities relating to emotion are known as joy, anger, melancholy, over-introspection, grief, fear and fright. These seven emotional factors are normal manifestations of a mental state under normal conditions, and they do not cause dominant physical changes in the body. However, if the mental stimulation is too intense and persistent, the body will fail to balance Yin and Yang, be unable to coordinate the Qi and blood circulation, will develop obstructions in the meridians and collaterals, and will develop dysfunctions in the Zang-fu organs. The anti-pathogenic factors are consumed, and disease occurs.

The seven emotional factors are endogenous and directly injure the five viscera: anger injures the liver; over-introspection injures the spleen, causing poor appetite; joy injures the heart, promoting blood-pressure problems and causing apoplexy; grief injures the lungs, causing hemoptysis. On the other hand, these same endogenous pathogenic factors also influence the normal circulation of Qi, joy slows the circulation; anger increases it; over-introspection focuses it; grief loosens it and fear or fright reduces it. Therefore, also because of these effects, the functions of Zang-fu organs cannot be properly maintained, and disease occurs.

Meridian Qigong exerts its influence by focusing the mind on only one thought instead of many thoughts, as it moves only the Qi along the meridians. Not only does the circulation of Qi regulate the mind and the function of the cerebral cortex but it adjusts the interaction among Zang-fu organs. Thus, if the transmission of Qi through the meridians is fluid, an improvement in mental state will result in a brighter outlook; diseases will be eliminated, and bodies will become stronger. These results will entail if the practitioner concentrates his mind and eases his thinking while practicing Meridian Qigong.

It has been reported that the electroencephalograms of those who suffer from diseases caused by these seven emotional factors manifest changes after practice of Meridian Qigong. The picture of a low amplitude, fast wave before practice changes into slow wave, and a poor-frequency wave pattern into a good one after practice. When practice has been persistent, the changes in the EEG show that the slow-frequency wave occurs and that its amplitude is three times higher than that of a nonpractitioner. These changes prove that Qigong prevents overstimulation and allows the pathogenic sites affected by seven emotional factors to recover. As a result, the functions of the central nervous system are improved, and the Zang-fu organs are regulated.

B. Inhaling and Exhaling: Regulation of Respiration
   Storage of Energy and Accumulation of Oxygen

Physical exercises such as basketball, gymnastics, and track and field sports all expend energy by accelerating the heartbeat and respiration and by making the muscles tense. But Qigong emphasizes ease, stillness, and regulation of respiration. Actually, practicing Qigong is a means of storing energy that is called "Nei Yang Gong" or internal body building. Practicing Qigong, with its conscious inhaling and exhaling, causes most of the 75 million alveoli to work. Gas exchange is efficient, so there is an increase of oxygen in the blood, and the metabolic activity of the cells is improved. Anti-pathogenic Qi becomes strong enough to remove diseases, thereby prolonging life.

C. Motion and Stillness: Activation of the Limbs by Massage to Regulate Energy

While practicing Qigong, motion and stillness exist simultaneously: Motion exists in stillness and stillness in motion; in the movement of the limbs there is strength as well as gentleness, just as in massage. Energy is regulated with the limbs being activated to circulate Qi through the meridians and collaterals by gently moving hands in coordination with feet, elbows with knees, shoulders with hips, and by massaging the points on the head and around the facial features. The motion stimulates the meridians and collaterals and promotes the functioning of their points. The results are that the mind is clear and eyes are bright.

The pressure within the abdomen is changed with slow, deep, regular inhaling and exhaling. As a result, the stomach and intestines are "massaged" at the same time. Therefore, Qigong exercise improves the digestive and absorptive processes and increases the secretions of digestive glands. After practicing, the appetite improves.

IV. How to Practice

The best time to practice Meridian Qigong is from five to seven o'clock in the morning or in the late afternoon. Then the environment is quieter, and there is more fresh air. The frequency of practice depends on the individual's condition. The elderly, sufferers of serious disease as well as persons in poor health should practice less, generally once or twice a day for 20 to 40 minutes each time. However, younger people, people with mild problems, and people in good health can practice more, twice or three times a day for 20 to 40 minutes each time. If the patient is in hospital, then the frequency should be decided upon by the doctors. A normal person should practice it at least once a day for 30 minutes immediately upon getting out of bed in the morning. The frequency and duration ultimately depend on body's response, and this Qigong should not be fatiguing.

The usual direction is to position oneself parallel to the magnetic lines of the globe towards south or north. One can also practice in the direction of the sunrise or towards the moon. Nevertheless, because man's adaptability is very strong, he need not be limited by conditions mentioned above. Success is the result of persistent practicing.

V. Notes on Practicing Meridian Qigong

A. Requirements Before Practicing

1. One should not be influenced or disturbed by the

environment. There should be no self-consciousness and no other-consciousness. One should remove all thoughts from one's mind and focus on moving the Qi through the meridians. The following is the process:

a) One thought instead of many thoughts will circulate the Qi through the 14 meridians and collaterals, beginning with the Lung Meridian and going to the Large Intestine Meridian, then to the Stomach, the Spleen, the Heart, the Small Intestine, the Urinary Bladder, the Kidney, the Pericardium, the Sanjiao, the Gall Bladder, and the Liver meridians and then back to the Lung Meridian; it then moves from the Ren Meridian to the Du Meridian.

b) Practicing Qigong requires one to move all joints and parts of the body gently in order to transmit Qi along the meridians, thereby generating the Qi energy properly. The movements are required to be graceful; there is a flow between motion and stillness; strength is practiced with gentleness, and ease and tension alternate.

c) One should breathe naturally, inhaling through the nose and exhaling through the mouth. The breathing should be slow, deep, gentle and even. One should not hyperventilate.

d) If there is a lot of noise or disturbance in the environment while one is practicing, one should continue with the practice, as if the distraction had not been seen or heard.

2. If possible, choose a peaceful environment where there are flowers and trees and the air is fresh. If the practice is to be carried out in a room, the room should be well-ventilated. In winter, take appropriate precautions against the cold.

3. This is Meridian Qigong, therefore, the practitioner should learn the distribution, flow routes, the connections with senses and orifices.

4. Before practicing, brush the teeth, wash the face and go to the toilet. The collar and belt should not be tight.

5. Qigong can be practiced on the edge of a bed or on a bench by those who are elderly or in poor health, suffer from chronic disease, or cannot stand. All other requirements are the same.

B. Requirements During Practice

Read the requirements for each of the 14 meridians in Chapter 3.

C. Requirements for Ending the Practice

1. The practice should end well. One should bend his knees, hold Qi in his arms, transmit Qi into the heart and pause. After that, lift the kidney Qi three times, lift the heels while deeply inhaling, and then put down the heels while exhaling. Relax every part of the body. If the practice should be interrupted, use the above method to end, lest discomfort occur.

2. Depending on the disease one can select which meridian(s) and collateral(s) through which best to exercise Meridian Qigong. One need not do all 14 sets of movements. Regardless, at the end of the practice, the method mentioned above should be followed.

D. Effects of the Practice

1. Immediate effects when the practice session has just ended

When the practice session has just ended, the subject feels that he can think quickly and clearly; he is in high spirits and relaxed; the senses of sight and hearing are heightened. Morning practice produces a good appetite and the ability to work energetically the whole day. The reason is that through Meridian Qigong one learns to focus his mind on the process of moving the Qi along the meridians and collaterals. Moveover, the breathing is deep and regular, so that the oxygen in the blood increases. Lastly, all the limbs and joints are moved and points on the head and around the features (eyes, ears, nose and mouth) are stimulated through massage.

2. Further effects (after practicing Qigong for one to three months)

After practicing for one month, one may expect the following conditions to improve: headache, dizziness, insomnia, and dreaminess, poor appetite, lack of strength, cough, shortness of breath, too much thick phlegm, low spirits, palpitations, tightness in the chest, menstrual disorders, impotence, premature ejaculation, lumbago, joint pain and poor memory. After two months' consistent practice, these conditions should be greatly improved or should have disappeared. Strength is renewed, the digestive function is enhanced, and edema is reduced. Those who are slower to recover and do not experience the expected effects should persist in practice, for changes will indeed come. After three months' practice, overall there will be effects on blood pressure, vision, brain, liver, kidney, and lung functioning; blood-oxygen level, the tongue, and pulse.

VI. Tailoring Meridian Qigong Practice to Particular Disorders

A practitioner is expected to master all the

movements of Meridian Qigong and to perform them with ease. Then he can select the meridians to concentrate on, depending on his state of health and the disease or disorder. Therefore, which and how many meridians and collaterals are used depends on the location of the disease. The following are given as examples.

1. The locations of neurasthenia, insomnia, amnesia, premature ejaculation, seminal emission, and impotence are in the Heart, Kidney, Ren and Du Meridians. So after practicing all the Qigong movements, the patients who suffer from these disorders should concentrate on these meridians. Attention should also be given the Small Intestine and Urinary Bladder Meridians, which internally and superficially relate to the heart and kidneys.

2. The locations of dyspepsia, chronic bronchitis, emaciation, and edema are in the Spleen Lung, Kidney and Ren Meridians. So after practicing all the movements, the patients who suffer from these infirmities should concentrate on these meridians as well as on the Large Intestine and Stomach Meridians, which internally and superficially also relate to the spleen and lungs.

3. The sources of early-stage hypertension, insufficient blood in the brain arteries, palpitations, edema, chronic hepatitis and chronic cholecystitis are in the Liver, Gall Bladder, Pericardium, and Sanjiao Meridians. So after practicing all the movements, patients who suffer from these problems should concentrate on performing again the movements of these meridians. Meridian Qigong can be practiced concurrently by those who are doing or have done

other forms of Qigong. However, we suggest practicing the "Quiescent Form" in order to relax the body. Then begin with the starting form to transmit Qi into the heart, and exhale and inhale deeply before practicing Meridian Qigong.

Starting Form

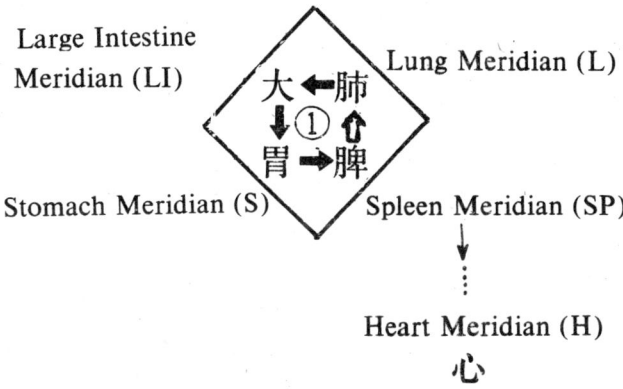

CHAPTER 2

STARTING FORM

I. Put Qi into Dantian

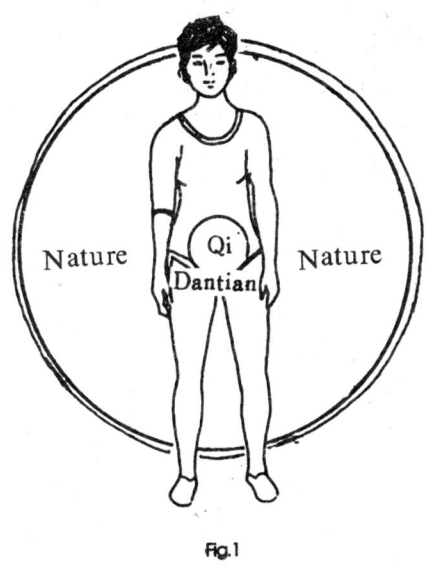

Fig. 1

Instructions:
1. Stand with feet apart (Fig. 1)

Keep the spine straight. Relax the body. Breathe normally. Do not square the shoulders or pull in the abdomen consciously. Keep the feet parallel and flat, spaced at shoulders width. Half open the eyes (neither closed nor open eyes are good for mental concentration.) Look straight ahead. Drop the arms to your sides naturally. Close the mouth gently and let the tip of the tongue touch the ridge behind the upper front teeth. Empty your mind of all distractions.

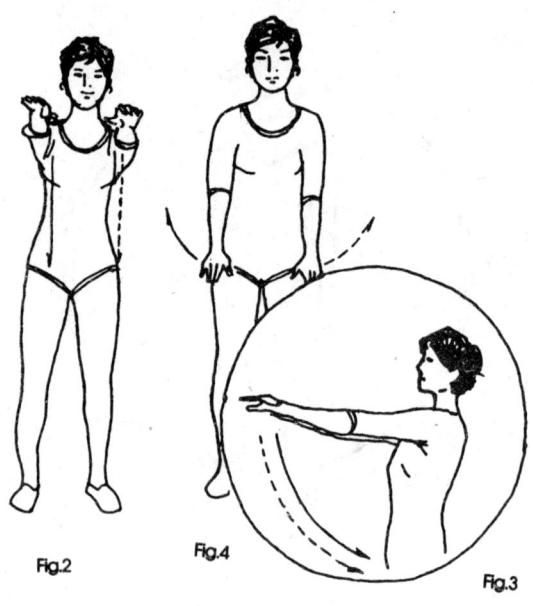

Fig.2 Fig.4 Fig.3

2. Raise the arms (Figs. 2, 3, 4)

While inhaling, slowly raise your arms in front of your body until they reach shoulder level.

3. Drop the arms (Fig. 2)

Press the arms to the front of pelvis slowly while exhaling.

4. Raise the arms to the sides (Fig. 4).

While inhaling, raise the arms slowly to your sides until they reach shoulder level.

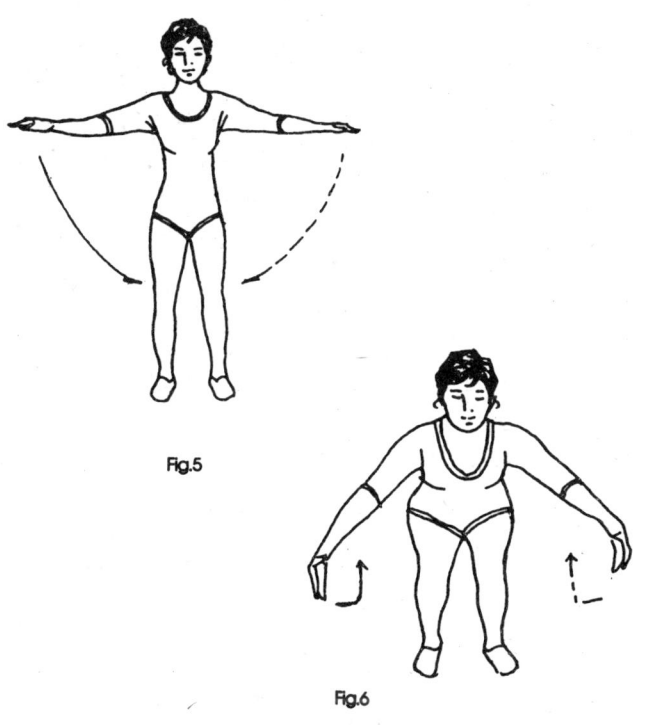

Fig.5

Fig.6

5. Bend the knees and hold the Qi (Figs. 5, 6).
While exhaling, bend the knees slowly until squatting. The arms seem to be holding a big ball.

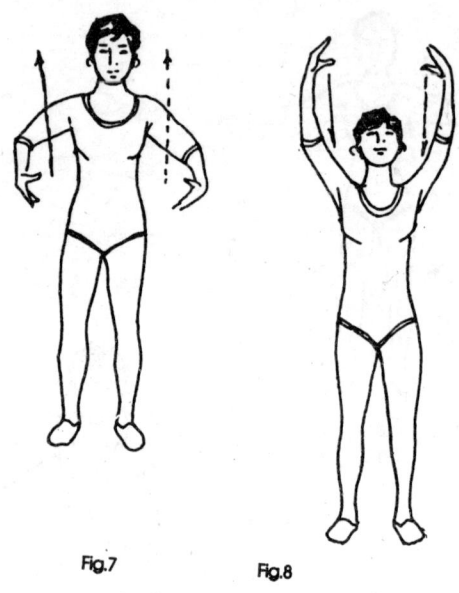

Fig.7   Fig.8

6. Straighten the body and lift the arms over the head (Figs. 7, 8).

While inhaling deeply straighten the body slowly and with the arms lift the ball slowly over the head.

7. Move the Qi downward and exhale the turbid Qi (Figs. 8, 9).

While exhaling, slowly move the arms and the hands holding Qi down and passing the face, neck and chest. The turbid Qi is expelled.

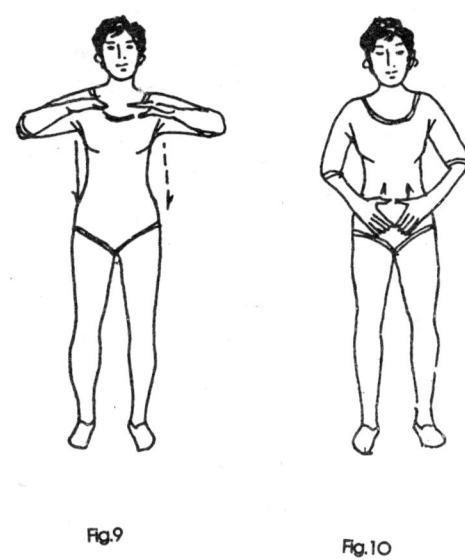

Fig.9 Fig.10

8. Concentrate on Dantian (Fig. 10).

Continue to push the Qi down to Dantian Concentrate on Dantian. Tense the abdomen, contract the muscles around the genitals and anus, and clench the teeth while breathing normally. Do this three times. That is called "lifting the kidney-Qi by internal movement."

Notes:

Broadly speaking, Dantian is the region that covers the Guanyuan point (R. 4) below the umbilicus, Qihai point (R. 6), Shimen point (R. 5) and Zhongji point (R. 3). Qihai is the heart of Dantian. In a narrow sense, Dantian is the area around the Guanyuan point. Here it is referred to in the broader sense.

Fig.11   Fig.12

II. Exhalation and Inhalation

1. Stretch the arms forward (Fig. 11).

With the palms up, slowly stretch the bent arms forward and raise them while inhaling slowly.

2. Look at the sky and stretch the arms to the sides (Fig. 12).

While inhaling slowly and deeply, stretch the raised arms all the way to the sides. At the same time raise the head and look up.

3. Straighten the body and join the hands (Fig. 12).

Straighten the body and gradually move the hands together over the head while inhaling slowly and deeply.

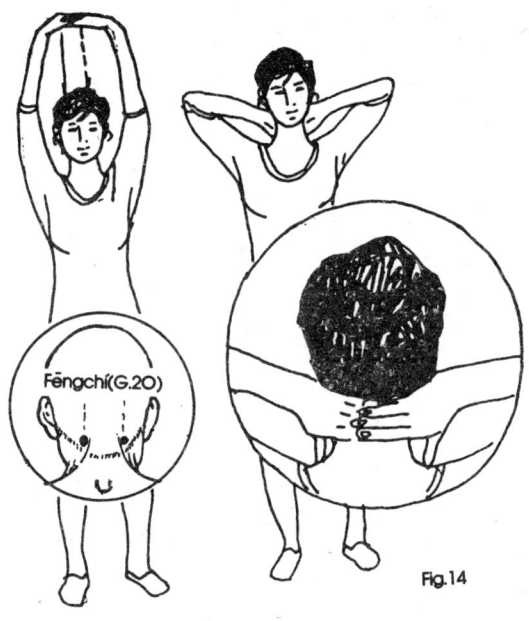
Fig.14

4. Lace the fingers high over the head (Fig. 13)

Overlap the fingers, except the thumbs, and stretch the arms over the top of the head. Usually the right hand is over the left one. Inhalation stops.

5. The Laogong point (P. 8) touches the Fengchi point (G. 20) (Fig. 14)

While exhaling, drop the hands to the occiput and make Laogong touch the Fengchi point.

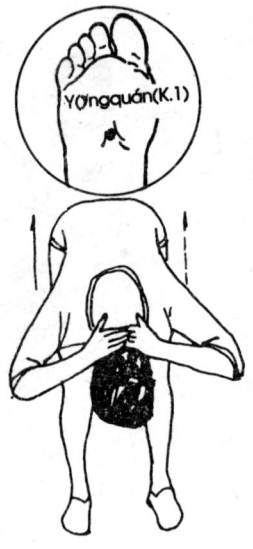

Fig.15

6. Inhaling and exhaling. Exhaling, concentrate on the Yongquan point (K. 1) (Fig. 15).

First breathe in. While exhaling slowly, keep your eyes straight ahead and bend forward until the eyes look at the ground. Concentrate on Yongquan until the exhaling is finished.

7. Inhaling and exhaling. Inhaling, concentrate on the Laogong point (P. 8) (Fig 16).

While straightening the body slowly, you will be aware of a stream of consciousness (Qi) that goes up to Laogong from Yongquan, along the lower limbs and back slowly. During the whole process, a deep and long

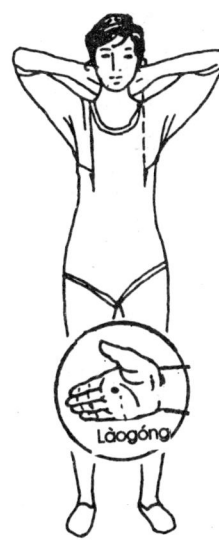

Fig.16

inhalation should be made. When the mind reaches the Laogong point, the inhalation should stop.

Notes:

The exhalation and inhalation exercises can be repeated several times. Usually three to nine times. For those who have weak lung-energy (Qi of the lung) or chronic diseases of the respiratory tract, such as chronic tracheitis and bronchitis, the actions may be repeated more than nine times. After the pure Qi (oxygen) and turbid Qi (carbon dioxide) have been exchanged, the practitioner will often feel much refreshed.

8. Separate the hands and drop the arms (Fig. 17).
Separate the hands slowly from the Fengchi point

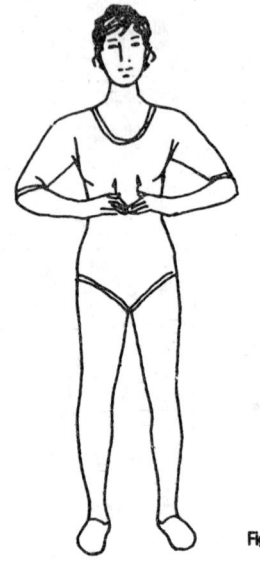

Fig. 17

(G. 20). Drop the arms slowly to the middle jiao, which is the starting position of the first of the twelve meridians the Lung Meridian of the Hand-Taiyin.

Keypoints:

One should exhale, while the Qi is being moved to the middle jiao. Pause and then concentrate on that position.

Notes:

The upper jiao: the spot between the diaphragm and the throat.

The middle jiao: the spot between the diaphragm and the umbilicus.

The lower jiao: the spot between the umbilicus and the pubis.

CHAPTER 3

THE 14 MERIDIANS

I. The Iung Meridian of the Hand-Taiyin

(Flow route): (Fig. L-1)

The Lung Meridian of the Hand-Taiyin originates from the middle jiao and runs downward to connect with the large intestine. Winding back, it goes along the upper orifice of the stomach, passes through the diaphragm, and enters the lung, its pertaining organ. From the portion of the lung that connects with the throat, it passes the nasal passages, spreads to the tongue, and then runs through the ears. Again from this same portion of the lung, the meridian proceeds transversely and descends along the anterior line of the medial aspect of the upper limb to the radial side of the tip of the thumb. The first point of this meridian is Zhongfu (L. 1); Shaoshang (L. 11) is the terminal point. The branch proximal to the wrist emerges from point Lieque (L. 7) and runs directly to the radial side of the tip of the index finger (Shangyang LI. 1) where it links with the Large Intestine Meridian of the Hand-Yangming.

Notes:

The meridian where it passes its pertaining organ is called "entering"; the code is "✘".

The meridian where it passes its connecting organ is called "connecting"; the code is " ⾡ ".

Indications:

Fullness and pain in the chest, cough, asthma, sore throat, pain in the shoulders and back, pain in the radial side of the forearm, irritability, hot palms (feverish sensation in the palms), abnormal rise in vital energy

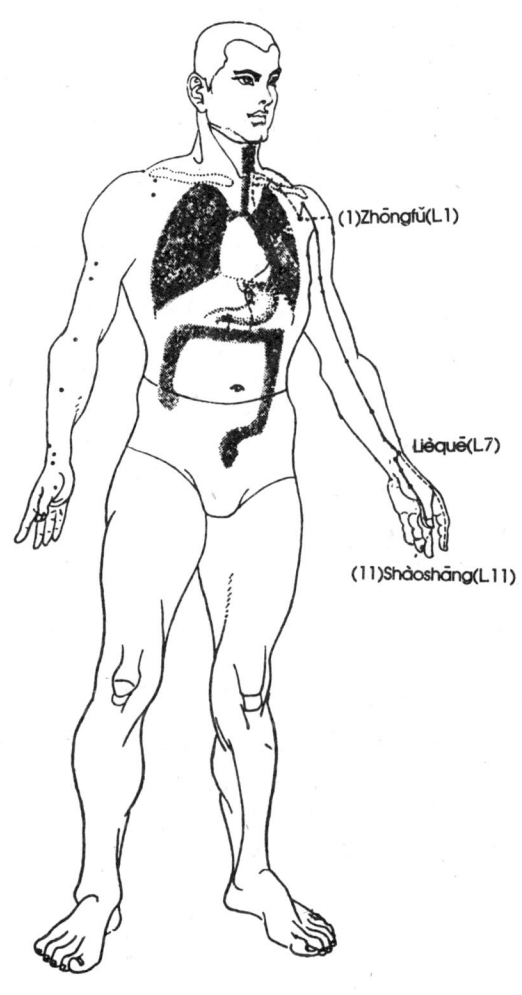

Fig.L-1　The Lung Meridian of Hand-Tàiyīn

Special indications:

Those who have bronchitis (not chronic) and often catch cold.

Requirements:

Concentrate on regulating the mind and respiration and moving the Qi along the meridians. Deep, long breaths should be taken. Remember Zhongfu (L. 1), Yunmen, (L. 2), Chize (L. 5), and Shaoshang (L. 11). The meridian goes from the chest to the head. Acupuncturists and Qigong masters should recite all the points along the meridian while moving the Qi along the meridian.

Location of the important points: (Fig. L.-2)

(Note: A Chinese cun is 3.3 millimeters, or slightly longer than an inch).

1. Zhongfu: Below the acromial extremity of the clavicle, 1 cun directly below Yunmen (L. 2).

2. Yunmen: In the depression below the acromial extremity of the clavicle, 6 cun to the side of the Ren Meridian.

5. Chize: On the crease in the elbow, on the radial side of the biceps brachii tendon.

7. Lieque: Above the styloid process of the radius, 1.5 cun above the transverse crease of the wrist. When the index fingers and thumbs of both hands are crossed, with the index finger of one hand placed on the styloid process of the radius of the other, the point is in the depression right under the tip of the index finger.

11. Shaoshang: On the radial side of the thumb, about 0.1 cun behind the corner of the nail.

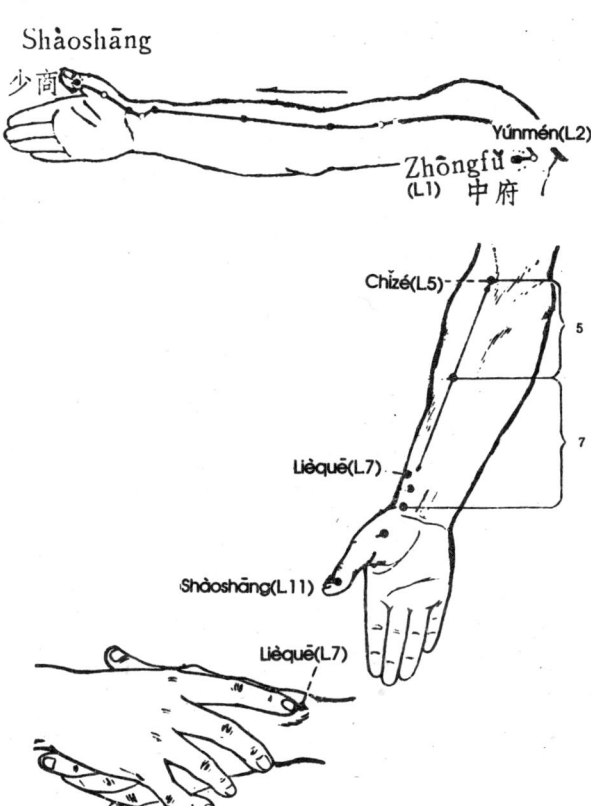

Fig.L-2 The Lung Meridian of Hand-Tàiyīn

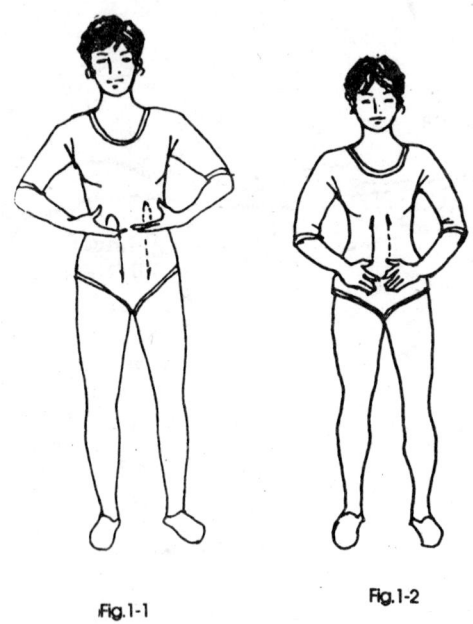

Fig.1-1 Fig.1-2

Instructions:

1. Start from the middle jiao (Fig. 1-1).

While inhaling, raise the hands slightly upward with the palms facing up.

2. Go down and connect with the large intestine (Fig. 1-2).

Turn the palms face down and, while exhaling, drop them slowly to the level of the large intestine.

3. Go back to the stomach (Fig. 1-3).

Turn the palms upward and while inhaling raise the hands slowly to the stomach.

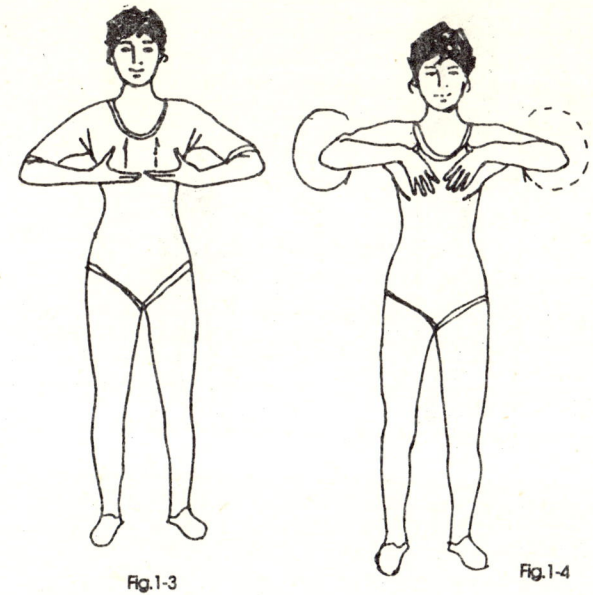

Fig.1-3 Fig.1-4

4. Pass the diaphragm and enter the lungs (Fig. 1-4).

While inhaling deeply, raise the hands past the diaphragm and make the palms and fingers touch the lungs.

5. Rotate the arms three times (Fig. 1-4).

As the hands touch the muscles of the chest, rotate the arms widely three times. Make the joints of shoulders, elbows and wrists move.

Keypoints:

While turning the arms, pay attention to the directions. First, while inhaling, the arms go downward and backward. Secondly, while exhaling, the arms go upward and forward.

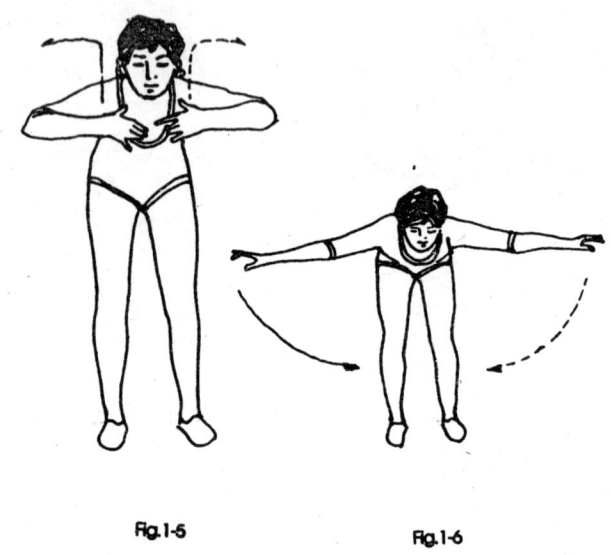

Fig.1-5   Fig.1-6

6. Opening into the nose, spread over the tongue and go through the ears (Fig.1-5).

The hands move the Qi upward from the lungs to the part connected to the throat. Concentrate on that as the Qi opens into the nose, spreads over the tongue and goes through the ears.

Keypoints:
Bend over gradually while slowly exhaling the turbid Qi.

7. Bend the knees and hold the Qi (Figs. 1-6, 1-7).

Stretch the arms out to the sides. While exhaling, bend over and squat. Stretch out the open fingers.

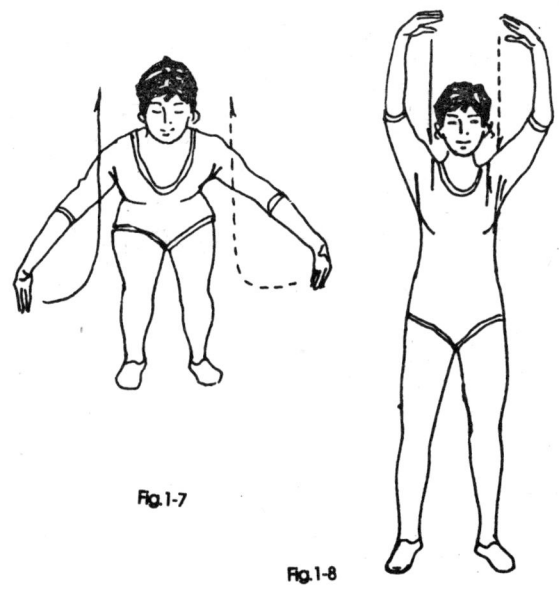

Fig.1-7

Fig.1-8

8. Straighten the body and lift the arms over the head (Fig. 1-8).

While inhaling deeply, straighten the body slowly, and with the arms lift an imaginary large, heavy ball slowly over the head.

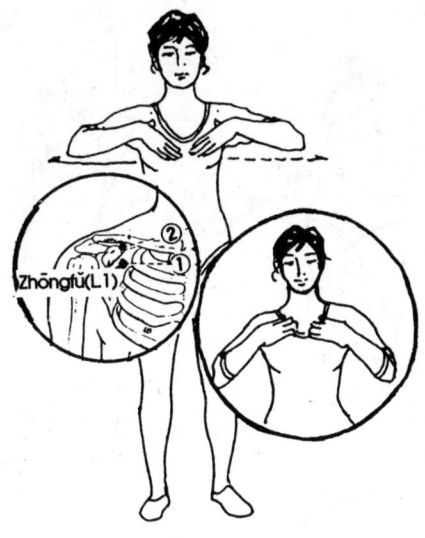

Fig.1-9

9. Pour the Qi into the lungs (Fig. 1-9)

While exhaling the turbid Qi, drop the raised arms slowly to the lungs. Put the palms on the lungs. Press Zhongfu (L. 1) with the thumbs and Yunmen (L. 2) with the index fingers.

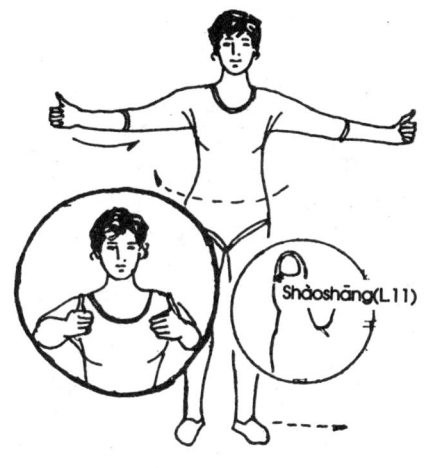

Fig. 1-10

10. Stretch the arms and extend the thumbs (Fig. 1-10).

While inhaling deeply, slowly stretch the arms out to the sides, simultaneously extending the thumbs and bending the rest of the fingers.

11. Go from the lungs to the hands (Figs. 1-10, 1-11).

Stretch the arms out wide. While inhaling slowly, concentrate the thoughts on the thumbs by passing the lungs and the anterior line of the medial aspect of the arms.

12. Turn the body to the right to move the Qi of the left side (Fig. 1-11)

Turn the trunk completely to the right. Put the weight on the right foot. Bend the right arm and put the fingers on Zhongfu point of the left side. Step one step to the left with the left leg.

13. Move the Qi along the left meridian (Figs. 1-12, 1-13)

Fig.1-12

Fig.1-11

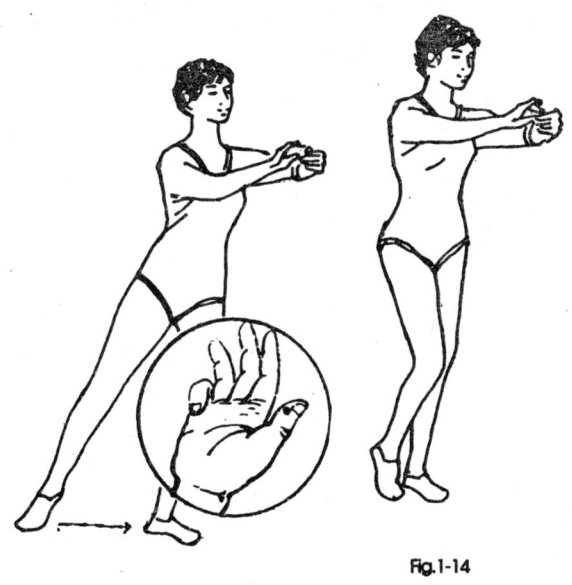

Fig.1-13

Fig.1-14

While exhaling slowly, turn the trunk gradually to the left. At the same time the right hand should move the Qi along the meridian, and the points should be read silently.

14. Bring the right foot together with the left foot (Figs. 1-13, 1-14). When the Qi has been moved to Shaoshang (L. 11), bring the right foot together with the left foot. While inhaling deeply, raise the arms and turn the trunk to the right. The weight shifts back to the right foot. The left foot takes a step to the left, and the right fingers return to Zhongfu. While exhaling, start moving the Qi of the left meridian. Move the Qi along the left meridian twice.

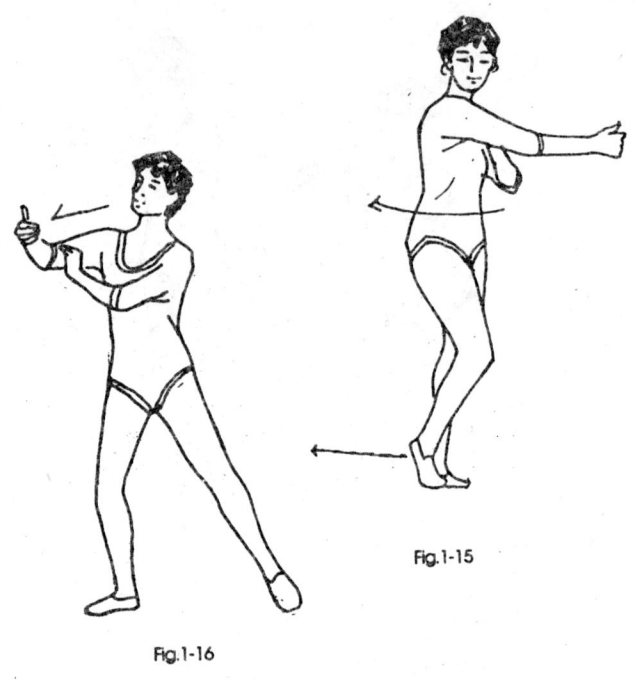

Fig.1-15

Fig.1-16

15. Move the Qi along the right meridian (Figs. 1-15, 1-16)

While inhaling, turn the trunk to the left completely. Bring the right foot together with the left foot. Shift the weight to the left foot and take a step with the right foot to the right. The left fingers should touch the right Zhongfu (L. 1). While exhaling slowly, turn the trunk to the right. At the same time the left hand should move the Qi along the meridian and the points should be read silently. Move the Qi along the right meridian twice (see action 14).

Fig. 1-17

16. Raise the arms and inhale (Fig. 1-17).

When the left hand gets to the right Shaoshang (L. 11), move the left foot until the feet are spaced at shoulder width. Raise the arms in an arc over the head while inhaling deeply.

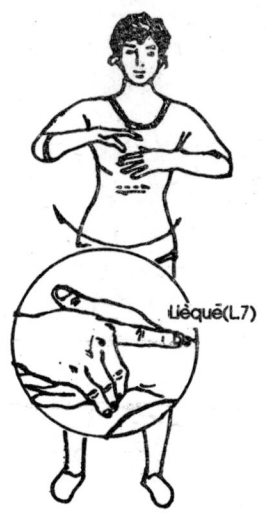

Fig.1-18

17. Move the Qi to the front of the lungs and crisscross Hukou (Fig. 1-18).

When the body is straight, move the Qi with the hands to the front of the lungs. Join hands between the thumbs and index fingers. Slowly exhale during this movement.

18. Lieque (L. 7) and Shangyang (L. 1) (Fig. 1-18)

After crisscrossing the hands, the index finger goes from Lieque to Shangyang. First do the left side with the right index finger. Then do the right side with the left index finger. Breathe normally. The Lung Meridian connects with the Large Intestine Meridian at the Shangyang points.

II. The Large Intestine Meridian of the Hand-Yangming

(Flow route): (Fig. LI-1)

The Large Intestine Meridian of Hand-Yangming starts from the medial side of the tip of the index finger (Shangyang LI. 1). Running upward along the radial side of the index finger and passing through Hegu (LI. 4), it goes upward along the lateral anterior aspect of the arm to the highest point of the shoulder Jianyu (LI. 15). From Jianyu it ascends to meet Dazhui (D. 14) then reaches the supraclavicular fossa. Two branches emerge. The internal one goes into the chest and connects with lung. Passing through the diaphragm, it enters the large intestine. The Qi from the large intestine terminates in Shangjuxu (S. 37). The superficial branch from the supraclavicular fossa runs upward to the neck, passes through the cheek and enters the gums of the lower teeth. Then it curves around the upper lip and crosses the opposite meridian at the philtrum. From there, the left meridian goes to the right and the right meridian to the left; the meridians go to both sides of the nose (Yingxiang LI. 20), where the Large Intestine Meridian links with the Stomach Meridian of the Foot-Yangming. The Qi at Yingxiang goes through the nose, spreads over the tongue and passes through the ears.

Indications:

Nasal obstruction, epistaxis, sore throat, runny nose, abdominal pain, diarrhea, constipation, pain in the shoulder and arm.

Fig.LI.-1

The Large Intestine Meridian of Hand-Yángmíng

Requirements:

Concentrate on regulating the respiration. While exhaling, move the Qi from the starting point to the elbow; while inhaling move the Qi from the elbow to Dazhui. The meridian goes from the hand to the head. There are altogether 20 points. Remember the starting point Shangyang and the ending point Yingxiang, besides Hegu, Quchi (LI. 11) and Jianyu (LI. 15). Acupuncturists and Qigong masters should recite all the points silently while moving the Qi along the meridian.

Location of the important points: (Fig. LI.-2)

1. **Shangyang:** On the radial side of the index finger, about 0.1 cun behind the corner of the nail.

4. **Hegu:** Between the first and second metacarpal bones, approximately at the center of the second metacarpal bone on the radial side.

11. **Quchi:** When the elbow is flexed, the point is in the depression at the lateral end of the transverse cubital crease.

15. **Jianyu:** Behindnd and below the acromion, in the middle of the upper portion of deltoid muscle.

20. **Yingxiang:** In the naso-labial groove, at the center of the outer side of the nostrils.

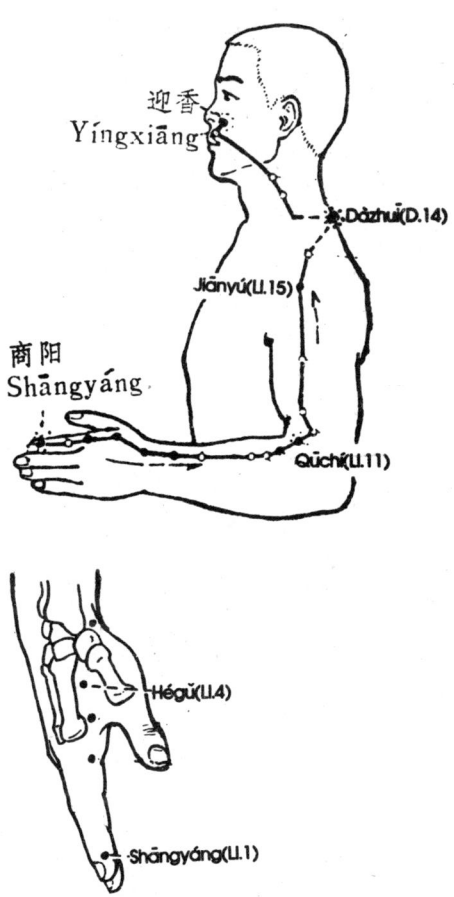

Fig.LI.-2 The Large Intestine Meridian of Hand-Yángmíng

Instructions:

1. Turn the body and stretch out the arms to the right (Fig. 2-1).

Turn the trunk and the right foot 90 degrees to the right. At the same time stretch the arms out to the right. Put the right index finger on the left index finger. The weight is on the right foot. Take a step backward with the left foot. Breathe normally.

2. Turn to the left to move the Qi of the left side (Fig. 2-2).

Gradually turn the trunk and the right foot 135 and the left foot 90 degrees to the left while moving the Qi along the meridian.

Keypoints:

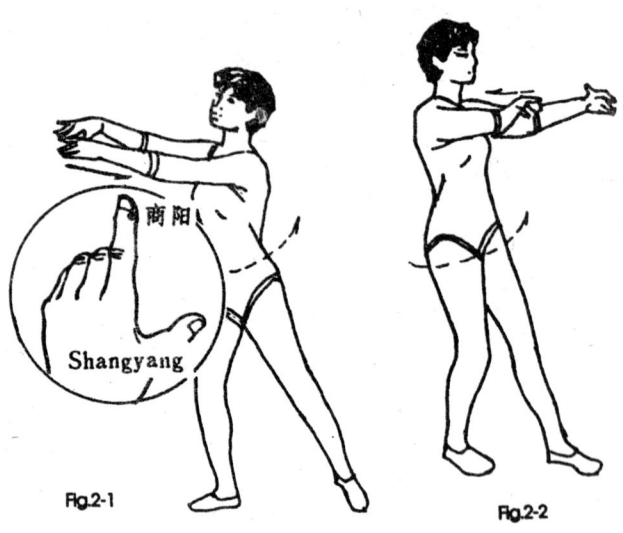

Fig.2-1 Fig.2-2

Fig.2-3

Fig.2-4

While exhaling, move the Qi from the beginning of the meridian to the elbow.

While inhaling, move the Qi from the elbow to Dazhui.

3. Reach Dazhui (Fig. 2-3).

When the Qi has been moved to Dazhui, bend the left arm. Turn the left foot 45 degrees to the left. Put the left index finger on the right index finger. Exhale during his movement.

4. Turn the trunk to the left and take a step forward with the right foot (Fig. 2-4).

While exhaling turn the trunk silightly to the left

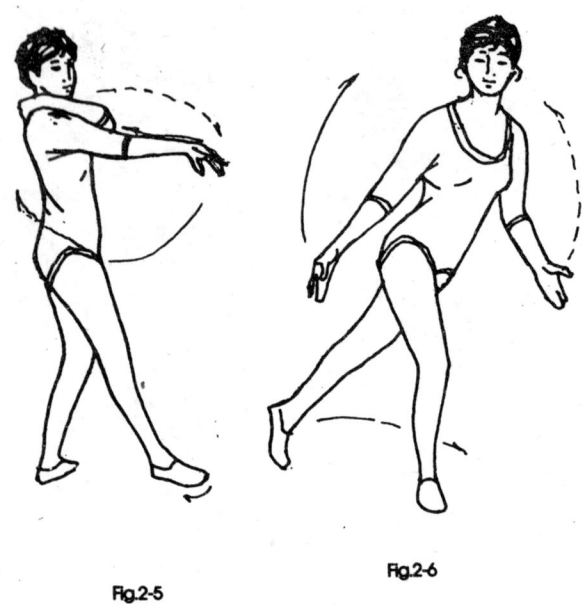

Fig.2-5

Fig.2-6

and take a step forward with the right foot. Stretch the arms out forward.

5. Turn to the right to move the Qi of the right side (Fig. 2-5).

Gradually turn the trunk and the right foot 45 degrees to the right while moving the Qi along the meridian to Dazhui. Put the right index finger on the left index finger. Take a step forward with the left foot. Again move the Qi in the left meridian.

Notes:

See the keypoints in action (2).

Move the Qi twice for each side.

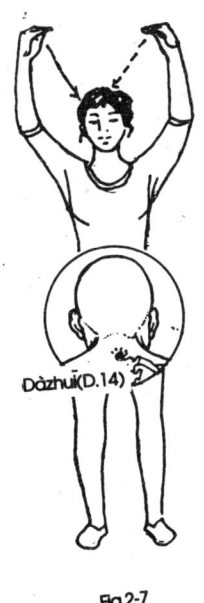

Fig.2-7

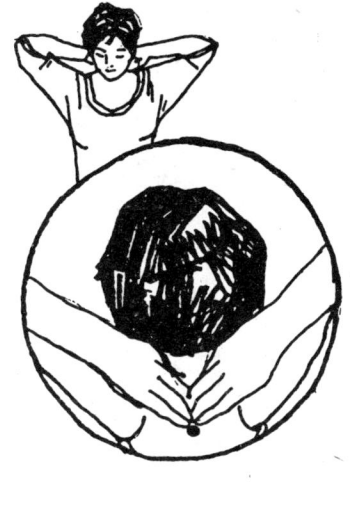

Fig.2-8

6. Turn the body and bring the fingers together (Figs. 2-6, 2-7)

Turn the body and the right foot 90 degrees to the right. Move the left foot so as to keep the feet as shoulders' width. While inhaling raise the arms from the back and bring the fingers together.

7. Touch Dazhui (Fig. 2-8).

While exhaling drop the hands to touch Dazhui.

8. Move Dazhui while nodding (Fig. 2-8).

Keep the body straight. Nod the head. Breathe normally.

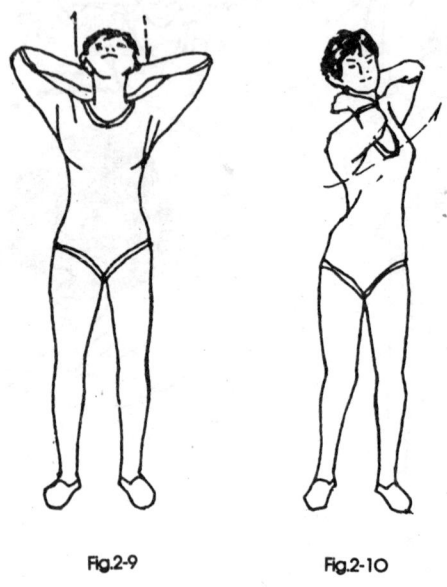

Fig.2-9   Fig.2-10

9. Move Dazhui while raising (Fig. 2-9).

Keep the body straight. Raise the head. Breathe normally. Do actions (8) and (9) six times in all.

10. Move Dazhui, turning to the left (Fig. 2-10).

Turn the trunk to the left and bend the knees. Straighten the knees and have the left elbow point downward and the right elbow upward.

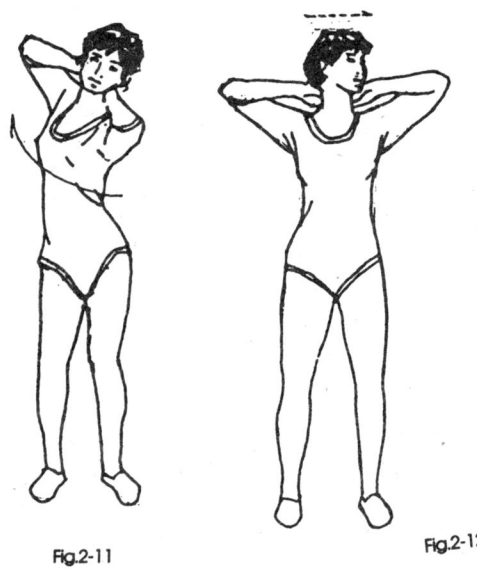

Fig.2-11　　　　　Fig.2-12

11. Move Dazhui, turning to the right (Fig. 2-11).

Turn the trunk to the right and bend the knees. Straighten the knees and have the left elbow point upward and the right one downward.

Notes: Actions (10) and (11) should move all the joints of the body.

Breathe normally during the exercises.

12. Turn Dazhui to the sides (Figs. 2-12, 2-13).

Keep the body straight. The hands are still on Dazhui. Turn the head to the left and right six times. Breathe normally.

13. Move to the supraclavicular fossa (Fig. 2-14).

Move the hands from Dazhui to the supraclavicular fossa. Breathe normally.

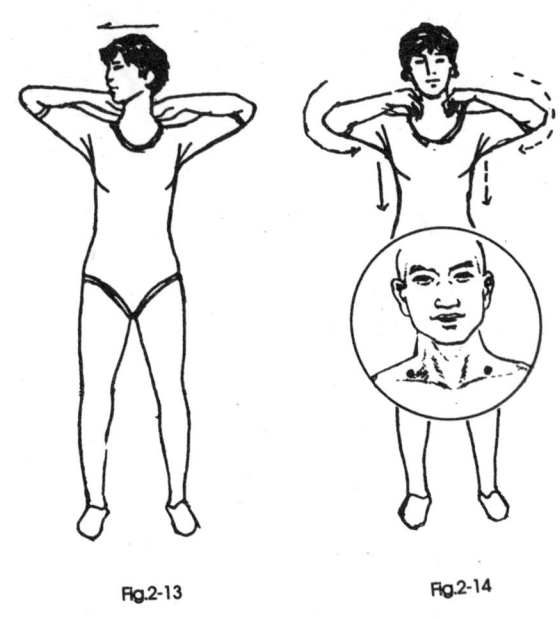

Fig.2-13   Fig.2-14

14. Rotate the arms three times (Fig. 2-14).

The fingers touch the supraclavicular fossa, rotate the arms from front to back three times. Breathe normally.

Notes:

While rotating the arms, relax the joints of the shoulders, elbows, wrists and fingers.

15. Go into the body from the supraclavicular fossa (Fig. 2-14).

While exhaling, drop the hands. The thoughts

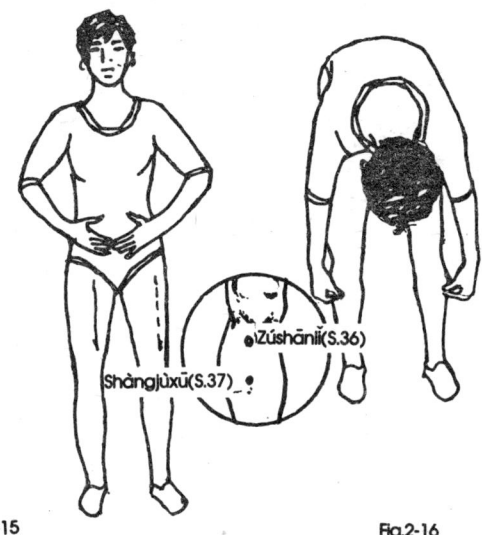

Fig.2-15   Fig.2-16

concentrate on the body.

16. Descend to connect with the lungs (Figs. 2-14, 2-15)

While exhaling, the hands reach the lungs. Pause, and the mind concentrates on the lungs, while they inhale.

17. Pass through the diaphragm and enter the large intestine (Fig. 2-15).

Drop the hands from the lungs. Passing through the diaphragm, the Qi enters the large intestine. Exhale during this movement.

18. Go downward to meet Shangjuxu (Fig. 2-16).

Breathe in deeply and raise the body slightly. While exhaling slowly, bend forward and move the hands to Shangjuxu (S. 37)

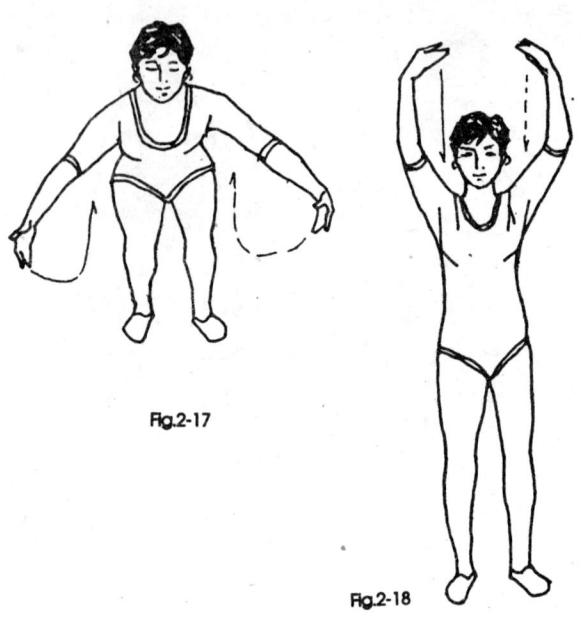

Fig.2-17

Fig.2-18

19. Bend the knees and hold the Qi (Fig. 2-17)
20. Straighten the body and lift the arms over the head (Fig. 2-18).

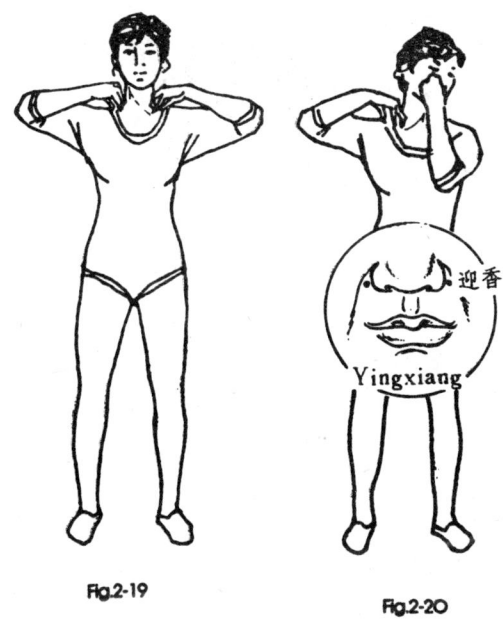

Fig.2-19 Fig.2-20

21. Pour the Qi into the supraclavicular fossa (Fig. 2-19)

While exhaling drop the hands to the supraclavicular fossa.

22. The left hand meets the right Yingxiang (Figs. 2-20, 2-21).

The left hand goes upward along the neck and the philtrum to the right Yingxiang (LI. 20) and then goes back to the original position. Breathe normally.

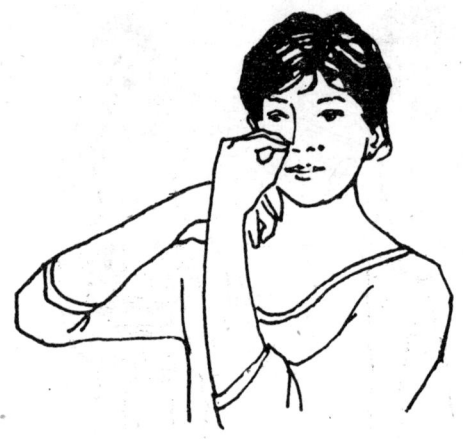

Fig.2-21

Fig.2-22

23. The right hand goes to meet the left Yingxiang (Fig. 2-22).

The right hand goes upward along the route to the left Yingxiang and then goes back to the original position. Breathe naturally.

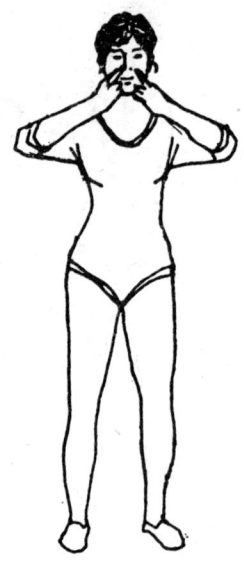

Fig. 2-23

24. Massage Yingxiang with the fingers six times (Fig. 2-23).

Cross the middle fingers onto the index fingers. Massage the Yingxiang (LI. 20) with them six times. There should be a sensation of slight soreness. Breathe normally.

III. The Stomach Meridian of the Foot-Yangming

(Flow route): (Fig. S.-1)

The Stomach Meridian of the Foot-Yangming starts from the lateral side of the nose, goes through the ear and spreads across the tongue. It ascends along the bridge of the nose and enters the inner canthus, where it meets Jingming (B. 1) and connects with the eye. Then it goes downward to Chengqi (S. 1), Sibai (S. 2) and Chengjiang (R. 24). It runs postero-laterally across the lower portion of the cheek at Daying (S. 5) and Jiache (S. 6). Ascending from the front of the ear, it reaches Touwei (S. 8). Descending from Daying to Qishe (S. 11) by passing Renying (S. 9), it moves posteriorly and meets Dazhui (D. 14). Turning forward, it enters the supraclavicular fossa, where the meridian separates into two branches. The internal branch runs downward from the supraclavicular fossa. It passes through the diaphragm, enters the stomach, its corresponding organ, and connects with the spleen. The meridian descends and enters Qichong (S. 30). The superficial branch runs downward, passing through the nipple. It descends by the umbilicus and enters Qichong. The two branches meet at Qichong. Descending along the anterior side of the upper leg, it reaches the knee. From there, it continues downward along the anterior line of the lateral aspect of the tibia to Chongyang (S. 42). From there, it reaches the lateral side of the tip of the second toe (Lidui S. 45). At Zusanli (S. 36) a branch emerges, and terminates at the lateral side of the middle toe. From Chongyang another branch emerges and terminates at the medial side of the tip of the big toe (Yinbai Sp. 1) where it links with the Spleen Meridian of the Foot-Taiyin.

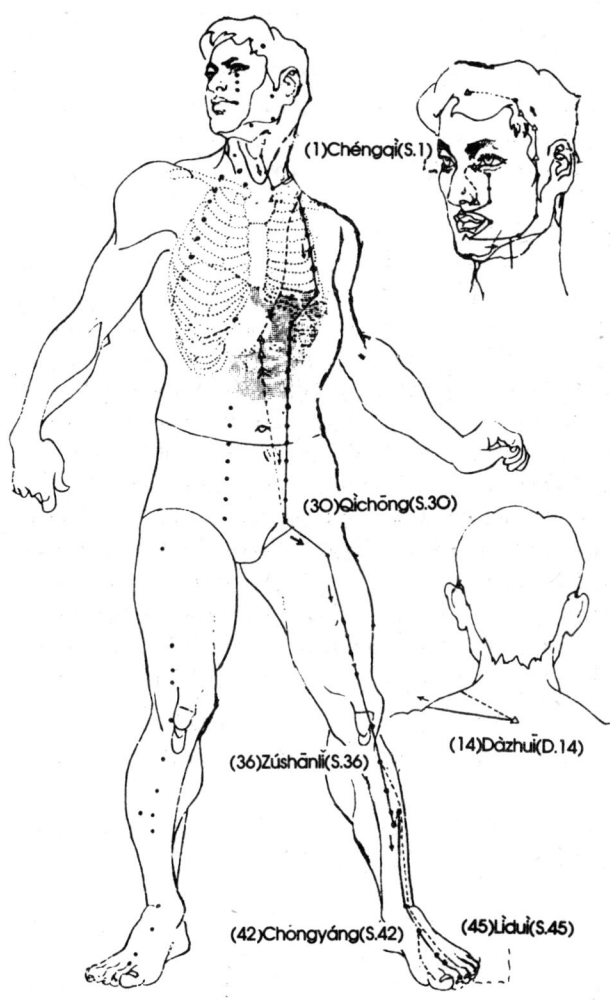

Fig.S.-1 The Stomach Meridian of Foot-Yángmíng

Indications:

Frontal headache, sore throat, abdominal distension, anorexia, diarrhea, pain in the lower back and knees, borborygmus, chronic gastritis, gastroduodenal ulcer, chronic colitis, anemia and hypertension.

Requirements:

When massaging the face, you should feel slight soreness and distension. Before massaging the face, apply cream to keep it soft and smooth and to make massaging more comfortable. Concentrate on regulating the respiration. When shaking Dazhui (D. 14), close the eyes and shake slowly. Those who have hypertension or cervical vertebrae problems should shake Dazhui more slowly. The Stomach Meridian goes from the head to the foot. Remember the sources of the three branches (supraclavicular fossa, Zusanli and Chongyang), the starting point Chengqi, the ending point Lidui, Qichong and Chongyang. Acupuncturists and Qigong masters should remember all the points, and recite them silently while practicing.

Location of the important points: (Fig.S.-2)

1. Chengqi: Between the eyeball and the midpoint of the infra-orbital ridge.
2. Sibai: Below Chengqi, in the depression at the infra-orbital foramen.
5. Daying: Behind the angle of the mandible, on the back edge of the masseter muscle, in the groove-like depression appearing when the cheek is bulged.
6. Jiache: One finger's breadth anterior and superior to the lower angle of the mandible where the masseter muscle attaches when the teeth are clenched.

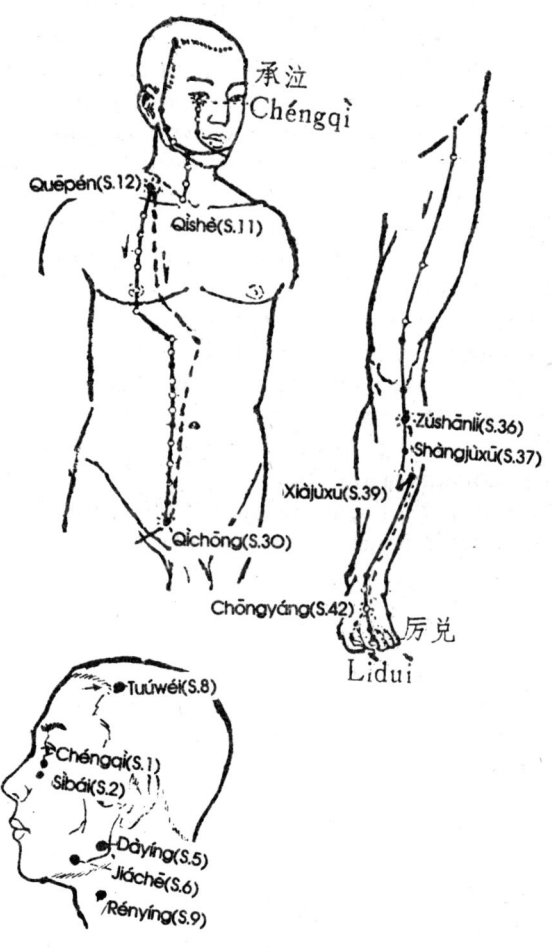

Fig.S.-2   The Stomach Meridian of Foot-Yángmíng

8. Touwei: 0.5 cun behind the front hairline at the corner of the forehead.

9. Renying: Level with the tip of Adam's apple, just on the course of the common carotid artery, on the anterior border of the sternocleidomastoideus muscle.

11. Qishe: At the superior border of the sternal extremity of the clavicle, between the sternal head and clavicular head of the sternocleidomastoideus muscle.

30. Qichong: Five cun below the umbilicus, 2 cun lateral to Qugu (R. 2), superior to the inguinal groove, on the medial side of the femoral artery.

36. Zusanli: Three cun below Dubi.

37. Shangjuxu: Three cun below Zusanli.

39. Xiajuxu: Six cun below Zusanli.

42. Chongyang: Distal to Jiexi, at the highest point of the dorsum of the foot.

45. Lidui: On the lateral side of the second toe, about 0.1 cun behind the corner of nail.

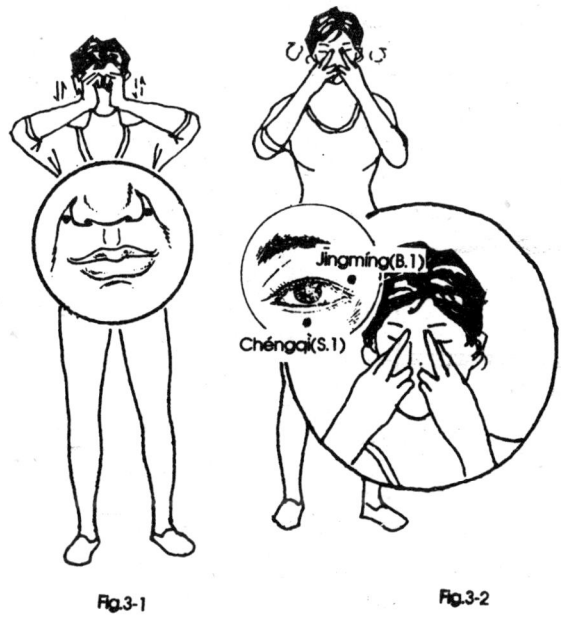

Fig.3-1 Fig.3-2

Instructions:

1. Massage Yingxiang with the thenars six times (Fig. 3-1).

Place the thenars (the bony projections at base of the thumbs) on the Yingxiang points and massage these points six times. Breathe normally.

2. Massage Jingming with the fingers six times (Fig. 3-2).

Put the middle fingers on the index fingers. Massage the Jingming (B.1) with the fingers six times. You should feel slight soreness.

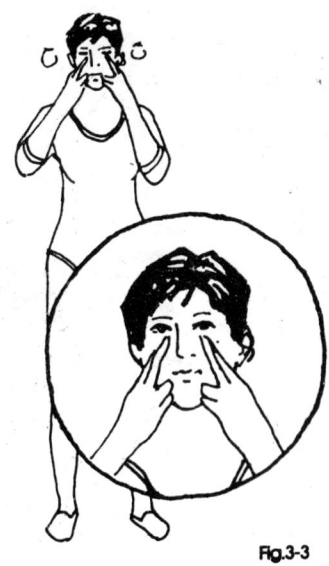

Fig.3-3

3. Massage Chengqi with the fingers six times (Fig. 3-3)

Massage Chengqi with the method mentioned above.

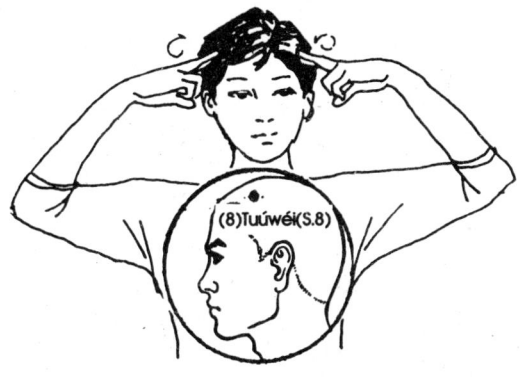

Fig.3-4

4. Massage the face six times (Fig. 3-4, 3-5)

After massaging Chengqi, the fingers move along the routes on the face until they reach the Touwei points. Massage the face along the routes with the palms six times. Breathe normally.

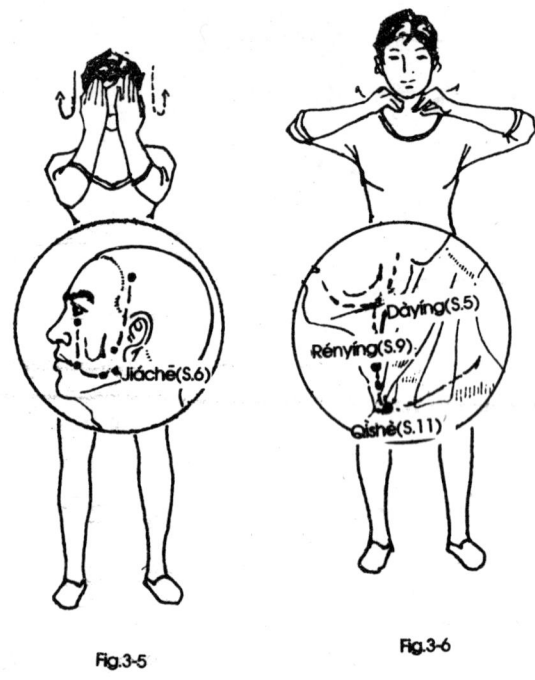

Fig.3-5 Fig.3-6

5. Descend from the face to Qishe (Fig. 3-6)

The fingers descend along the routes to Qishe (S. 11) and go backward to meet Dazhui (D. 14). Breathe normally.

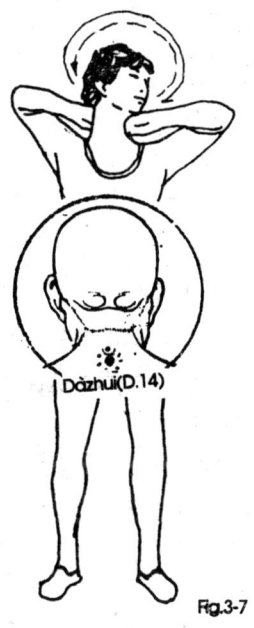

Fig.3-7

6. Rotate Dazhui six times (Fig. 3-7)

The fingers touch Dazhui. Rotate the head and Dazhui clockwise six times and then counterclockwise six times. Breathe normally.

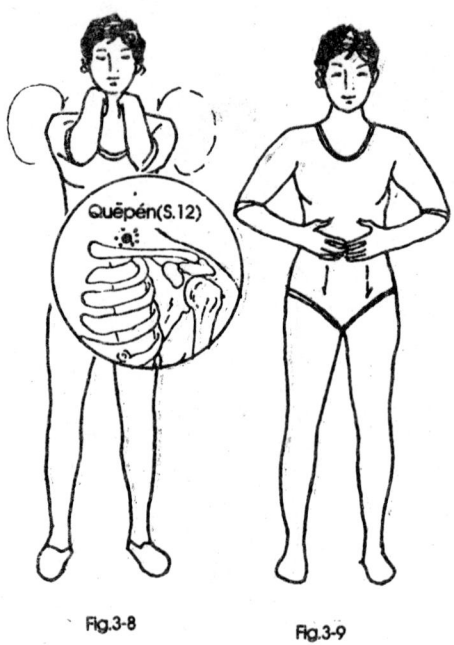

Fig.3-8   Fig.3-9

7. Go to the supraclavicular fossa and rotate the arms six times (Fig. 3-8)

Move the hands from Dazhui to the supraclavicular fossa. Rotate the arms six times. At the supraclavicular fossa, the meridian becomes two branches. First, move the Qi in the internal branch; then move the Qi in the superficial one.

8. Pass through the diaphragm, enter the stomach and connect with the spleen (Fig. 3-9)

The hands move downward from the fossa. Passing through the diaphragm, they move to the stomach and then connect with the spleen.

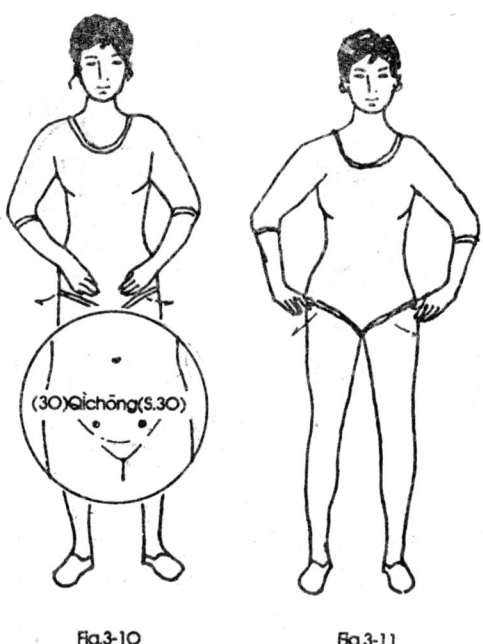

Fig.3-10　　　　Fig.3-11

Notes:

When the hands have moved the Qi to the stomach, a short pause should be taken. Then move downward to connect with the spleen. Exhale during this movement.

9. Go down to Qichong (Fig. 3-10).

The hands move the Qi to Qichong (S. 30). While inhaling, move the hands apart to the sides.

10. Bend the knees and hold the Qi (Figs. 3-11, 3-12)

While exhaling bend forward and squat. Stretch out the open fingers. Imagine that the arms are holding a big ball.

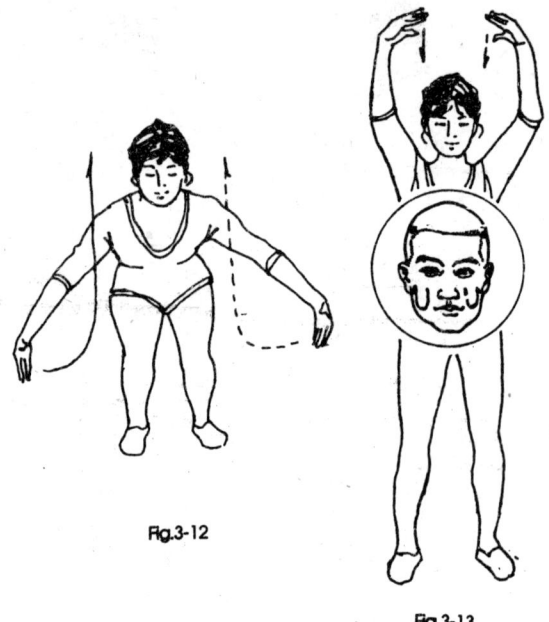

Fig.3-12

Fig.3-13

11. Straighten the body and lift the arms over the head (Fig. 3-13).

While inhaling deeply, straighten the body slowly and with the arms lift the ball slowly over the head.

12. Massage the face three times (Figs. 3-5, 3-13).

While exhaling drop the hands to the face. Massage the face along the routes three times. Breathe normally.

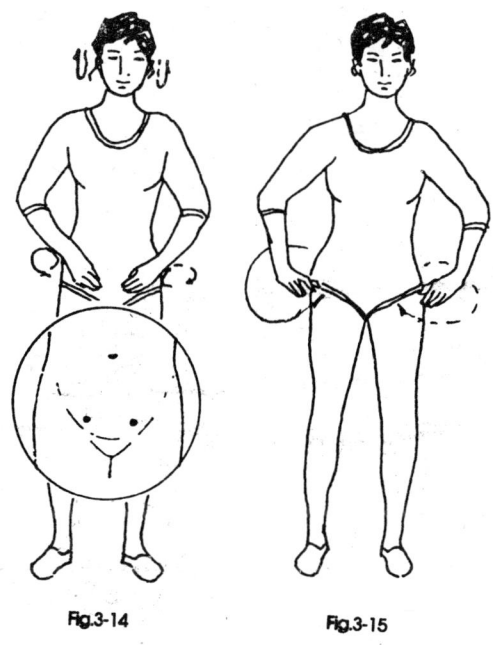

Fig.3-14   Fig.3-15

13. The Qi in the two branches meets at Qichong (Figs. 3-14, 3-15).

While exhaling slowly, the hands move downward from the face along the routes to Qichong where the Qi in two branches meets. In order to mix the Qi, the hands draw three circles in front of the pelvis. Breathe normally.

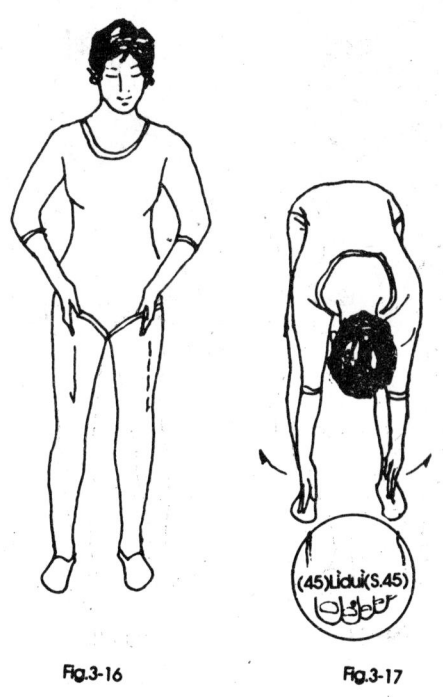

Fig.3-16   Fig.3-17

14. Reach the lateral side of the second toe (Figs. 3-16, 3-17).

Raise the shoulders and heels a little while inhaling deeply. While slowly exhaling, bend over, and at the same time move the Qi downward from Qichong along the routes. The Qi should reach Lidui (S. 45) at the lateral side of the second toes. If you cannot touch your toes, in your mind visualize touching them.

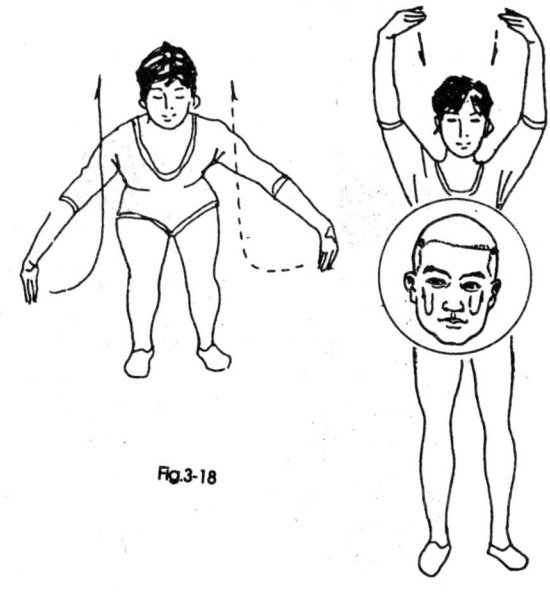

Fig.3-18

Fig.3-19

15. Repeat the actions in steps (10), (11), (12) and (13) (Fig. 3-18, 3-19)

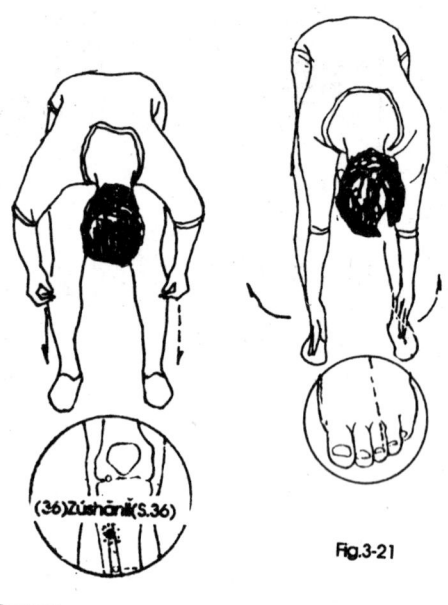

Fig.3-20

Fig.3-21

16. **Reach Zusanli (S. 36) (Figs. 3-20).**

Then move the hands downward along the routes to Zusanli (Figs. 3-18, 3-19). Pause. While exhaling, continue moving the hands downward along the branch routes.

17. **End at the lateral side of the third toes (Fig. 3-21).**

End at the lateral side of the third toes while exhaling fully.

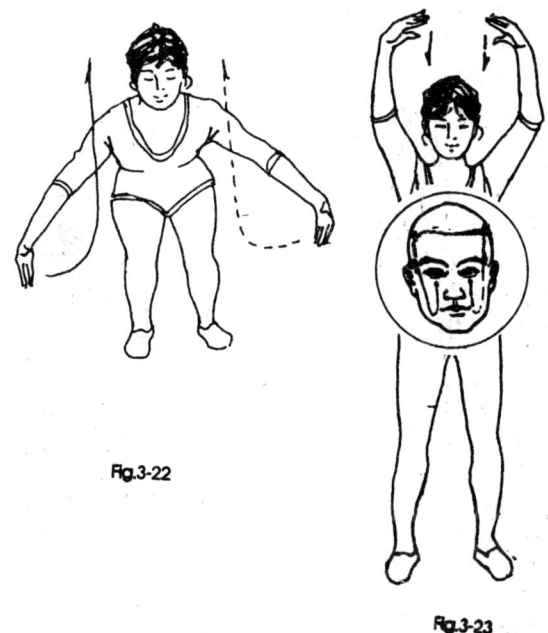

Fig.3-22

Fig.3-23

18. Repeat the actions in steps (10), (11), (12) and (13) (Figs. 3-22, 3-23).

19. Go down to Chongyang (S. 42) (Figs. 3-24, 3-25).

While exhaling, with the hands move the Qi along the route to Chongyang, where a branch emerges.

20. Terminate at Yinbai (Sp. 1) (Fig. 3-25, 3-26).

While exhaling, move the Qi along the branch and terminate at Yinbai, the medial side of the tip of the big toes, where it links with the Spleen Meridian of the Foot-Taiyin.

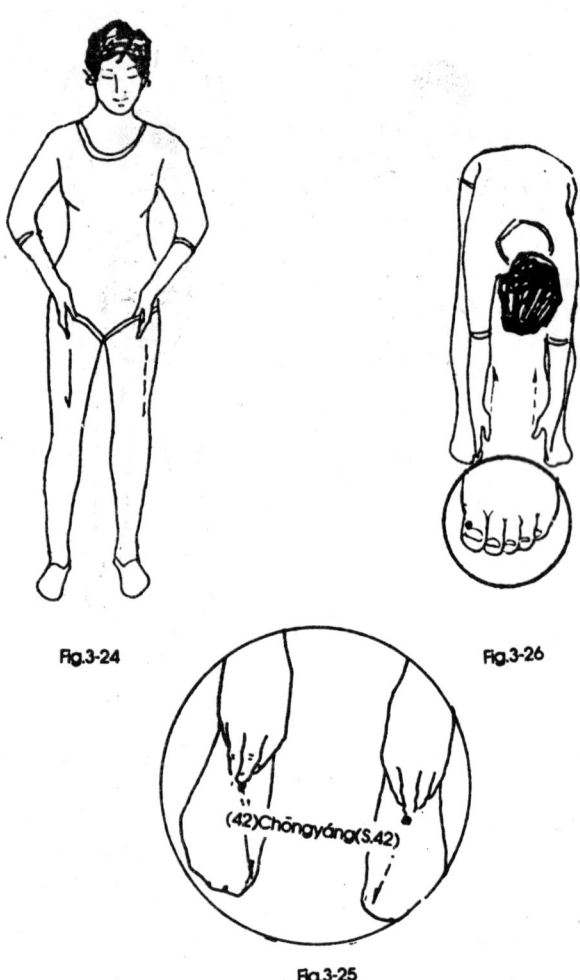

Fig.3-24

Fig.3-26

(42)Chōngyáng(S.42)

Fig.3-25

IV. The Spleen Meridian of the Foot-Taiyin

(Flow route): (Fig. Sp.-1)

The Spleen Meridian of the Foot-Taiyin starts at the tip of the big toe (Yinbai Sp. 1). It runs along the medial aspect of the foot at the junction of the darker and lighter skin and ascends in front of the medial ankle up the leg. There it follows the posterior aspect of the tibia, crosses and goes in front of the Liver Meridian of the Foot-Jueyin. It goes to Yinlingquan (Sp. 9). Passing through the anterior medial aspect of the knee and thigh, it enters the abdomen. At Chongmen (Sp. 12), it becomes two branches. The superficial one ascends along the route to Dabao (Sp. 21). The internal one enters the spleen, its pertaining organ, and connects with the stomach. From there is ascends, traversing the diaphragm, passing through the chest and running alongside the esophagus. It opens into the mouth, links with the ears and spreads over the tongue. The branch from the stomach goes upward through the diaphragm, and flows into the heart, where it links with the Heart Meridian of the Hand-Shaoyin.

Indications:

Sluggishness, anorexia, vomiting, abdominal distension, loose stools, chronic gastritis, gastroduodenal ulcer, anemia, and pain and soreness along the meridian.

Requirements:

While practicing, concentrate on regulating the respiration and mastering balance. Beginners should be able to control the center of gravity after practice. This can strengthen the balance center of the cerebellum.

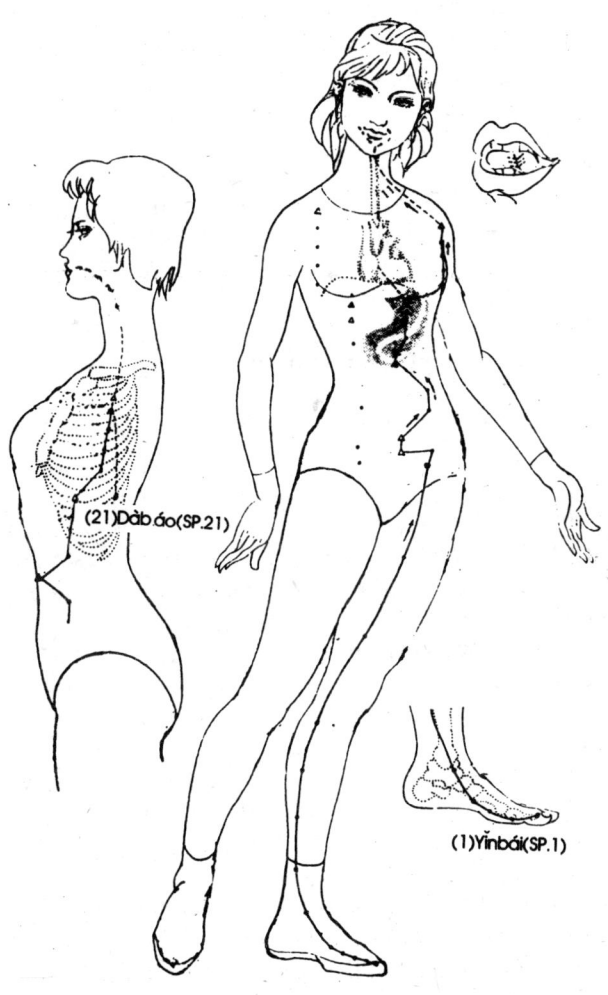

Fig.Sp.-1 The Spleen Meridian of Foot-Tàiyīn

For all the Foot Yin meridians, first move the Qi along the superficial branch and then along the internal one.

The Spleen Meridian goes from the foot to the chest. At Chongmen (Sp. 12) and the stomach, two branches emerge. There are 21 points in all. Remember the starting point Yinbai and the ending point Dabao (Sp. 21), as well as Sanyinjiao (Sp. 6), Yinlingquan (Sp. 9). Chongmen (Sp. 12) and Zhourong (Sp. 20). Acupuncturists and Qigong masters should recite all the points silently while moving the Qi.

Location of the important points: (Fig. p.-2)

1. Yinbai: On the medial side of the big toe, about 0.1 cun posterior to the corner of the nail.

6. Sanyinjiao: Three cun directly above the tip of the medial malleolus, on the posterior border of the tibia, on the line drawn from the medial malleolus to Yinlingquan (Sp. 9).

9. Yinlingquan: On the lower border of the medial condylus of the tibia, in the depression between the posterior border of the tibia and the gastrocnemius muscle.

12. Chongmen: Above the lateral end of the inguinal groove, on the lateral side of the femoral artery, at the level of the upper border of symphysis pubis, 3.5 cun lateral to Qugu (R. 2).

20. Zhourong: One rib above Xiongxiang (Sp. 19), directly below Zhongfu (L. 1) and Yunmen (L. 2), in the second intercostal space, 6 cun lateral to the Ren Meridian.

21. Dabao: On the mid-axillary line, 6 cun below the axilla, midway between the axilla and the free end of the eleventh rib.

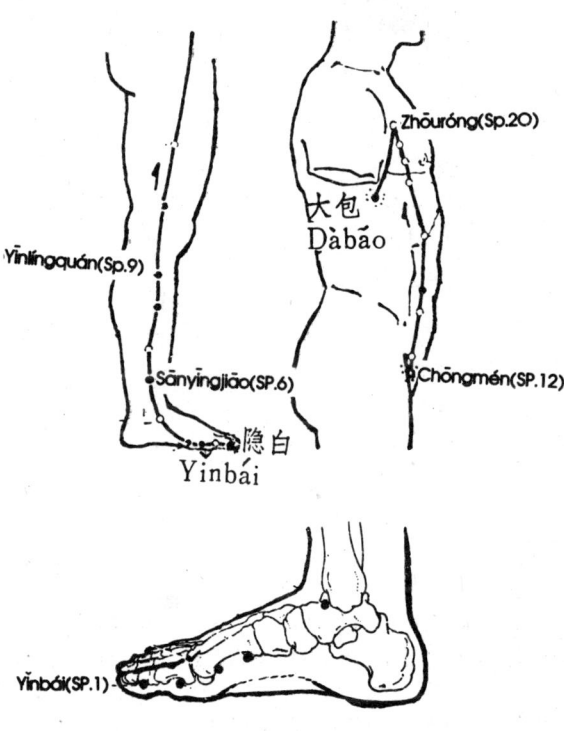

Fig.Sp.-2   The Spleen Meridian of Foot-Tàiyīn

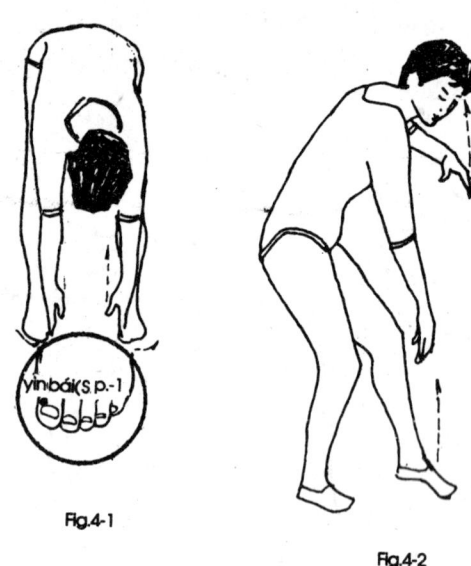

Fig.4-1

Fig.4-2

Instructions:

1. Turn the body to the left and move the Qi along the route of the left side (Figs. 4-1, 4-2, 4-3).

Slowly straighten the body from a bending position. Turn the trunk to the left. Turn the right foot 45 and the left foot 90 degrees to the left. Raise the left arm and leg. At the same time stretch the right arm to the left starting point Yinbai. If the hands cannot touch the point, concentrate on it. Move the Qi upward along the route. Inhale during the upward movement of the Qi.

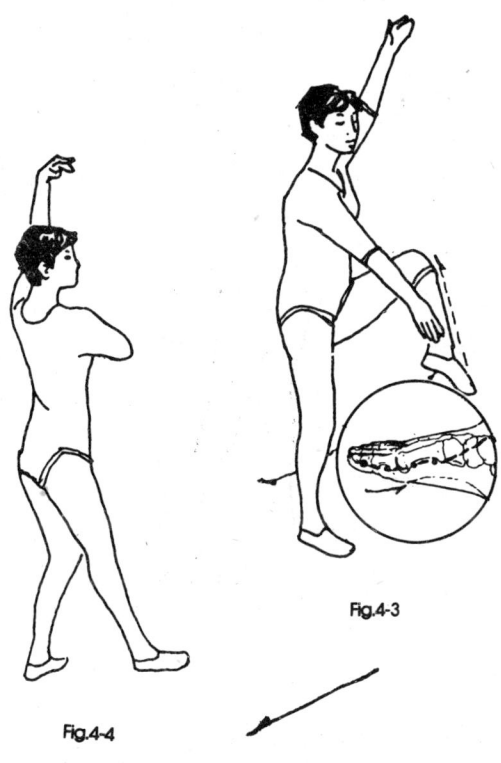

Fig.4-3

Fig.4-4

2. Move the Qi along the left side and take a step backward with the left foot (Fig. 4-4).

As the Qi is moved over the knee, take a step backward with the left foot. The right hand should continue to move the Qi upward. Pause after the Qi is moved to Chongmen (Sp. 12). Then continue to move it upward along the meridian. Inhale during the whole process.

Fig.4-5

3. Move the Qi along the left side to Dabao (Fig. 4-5). When the Qi has reached the Zhourong point (Sp. 20), turn the trunk slightly to the left and simultaneously move the Qi to Dabao (Sp. 21). At this point the inhalation should stop. Then return the trunk to the original position and gradually drop the left arm while exhaling.

Fig.4-6

4. Move the Qi along the right side and take a step backward with the right foot (Fig. 4-6).

While exhaling raise the right arm and leg and stretch the left arm to the right starting point Yinbai (Sp. 1). Start inhaling and move the the Qi upward along the route. As the Qi is moved over the knee, take a step backward with the right foot. The Qi continues to move up.

5. Move the Qi along the right side to Dabao.

When the Qi has reached the Zhourong point (Sp. 20), turn the trunk slightly to the right and simultaneously move the Qi to Dabao (Sp. 21). At this point the inhalation should stop. While exhaling, return the trunk to the original position and drop the

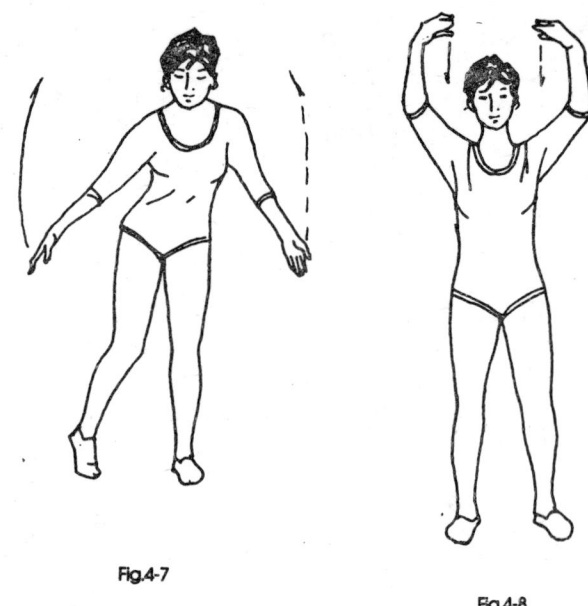

Fig.4-7

Fig.4-8

right arm slowly. Move the Qi twice along the meridian of each side.

6. Turn the body and raise the arms (Figs. 4-7, 4-8).

While exhaling and moving the arms down and to the back, turn the body to the right. While inhaling, gradually raise the arms from this postero-lateral position. Move the right foot so as to keep the feet at shoulders width.

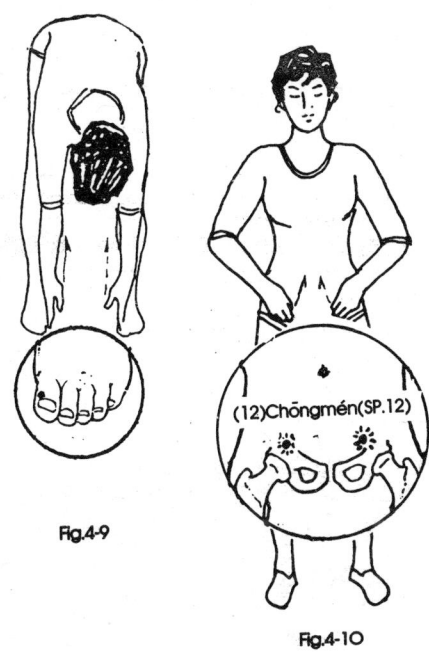

Fig.4-9

Fig.4-10

7. Move the bilateral Qi (Fig. 4-9).

While exhaling deeply, bend forward and with the hands touch the starting points Yinbai. While inhaling deeply, with the hands move the Qi upward along the routes, slowly straightening the body.

8. The Qi enters the abdomen from Chongmen (Sp. 12) (Fig. 4-10).

When the Qi has reached Chongmen, pause. Then while exhaling concentrate on moving the Qi into the abdomen.

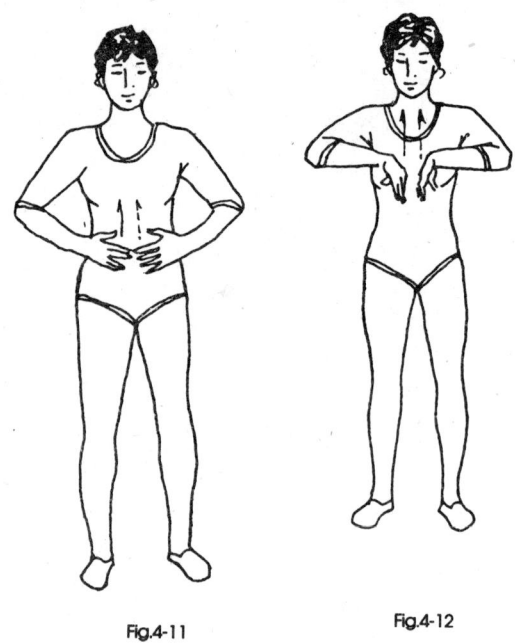

Fig.4-11   Fig.4-12

9. The Qi enters the spleen and connects with the stomach (Fig. 4-11)

Move the Qi upward until it enters the spleen and connects with the stomach. Breathe naturally.

10. Cross the diaphragm and run alongside the esophagus (Fig. 4-12).

While inhaling deeply, the hands cross the diaphragm and go through the chest, running alongside the esophagus.

Fig.4-13

11. Open into the mouth (Fig. 4-13).

Place the index fingers above and below the lips. Rub back and forth six times while visualizing the Qi spreading over the tongue and linking with the ears. Breathe normally.

12. Hold the Qi and move the bilateral Qi (Figs. 4-14, 4-15, 4-16, 4-17).

Bend the knees and hold the Qi.
Straighten the body and lift the arms over the head.
Move the bilateral Qi.
Repeat actions (8) and (9). (Figs. 4-10, 4-11).

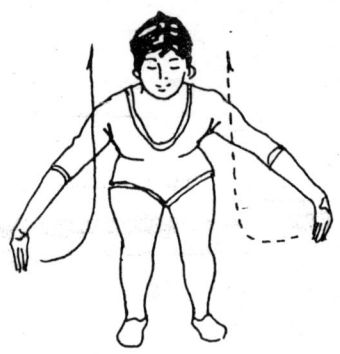

Fig.4-14

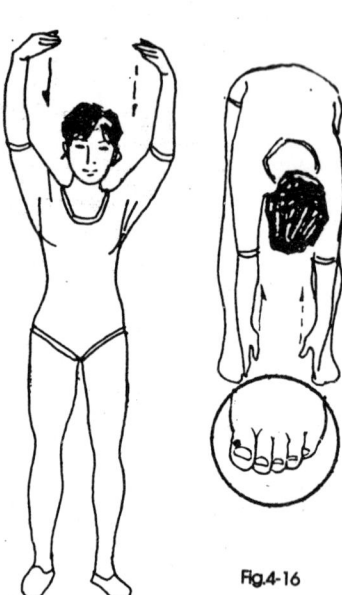

Fig.4-15

Fig.4-16

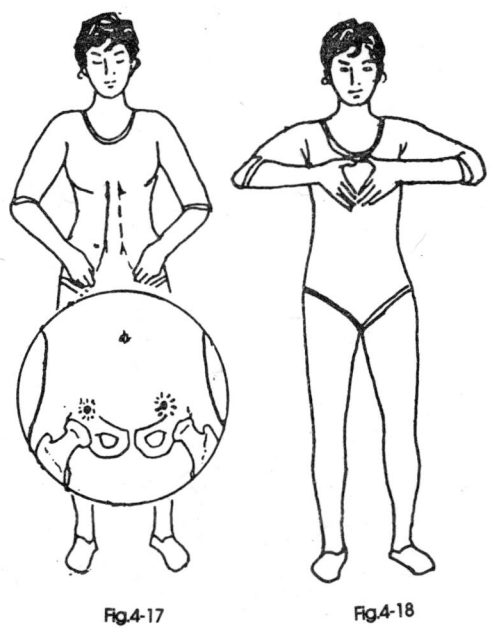

Fig.4-17   Fig.4-18

13. Flow into the heart (Fig. 4-18)
After a short pause, with the hands move the Qi in the stomach upward along the route. Move it through the diaphragm until it flows into the heart. Here it links with the Heart Meridian of the Hand- Shaoyin. Breathe normally.

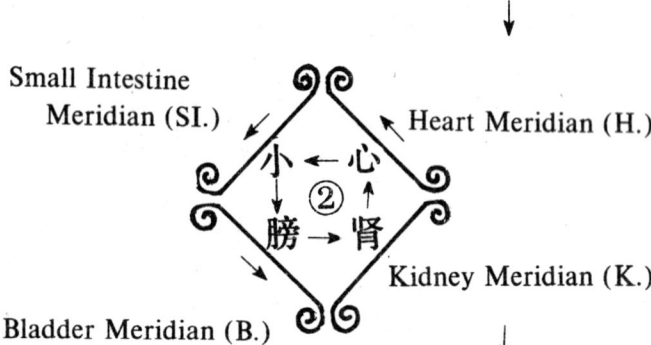

V. The Heart Meridian of the Hand-Shaoyin

Flow route: (Fig. P.-1)

The Heart Meridian of the Hand-Shaoyin starts from the heart. Passing through the diaphragm it connects with the small intestine. After going back to the "heart system" (i.e. the vessels connecting the heart with the other Zang-fu organs), it runs alongside the esophagus linking with the eyes, enters the brain and goes through the ears. It opens onto and spreads over the tip of the tongue. From the "heart system" it goes upward to the right lung. Then it extends laterally and emerges from the axilla (Jiquan H. 1). From there it goes along the posterior border of the medial aspect of the upper arm. Passing through Shaohai (H. 3) and Shengmen (H. 7), it reaches the medial tip of the small finger (Shaochong H. 9), where it links with the Small Intestine Meridian of the Hand-Taiyang.

Indications:

This meridian is used primarily to treat disorders of the nervous system and the cardiovascular system, such as arrhythmia, tachycardia, bradycardia, mild stenocardia, sore throat, insomnia, pain in the chest and hypochondrial region, feverish sensation in the palms, deficiency of circulation to the heart, dream-disturbed sleep and pain along the posterior border of the medial aspect of the arms.

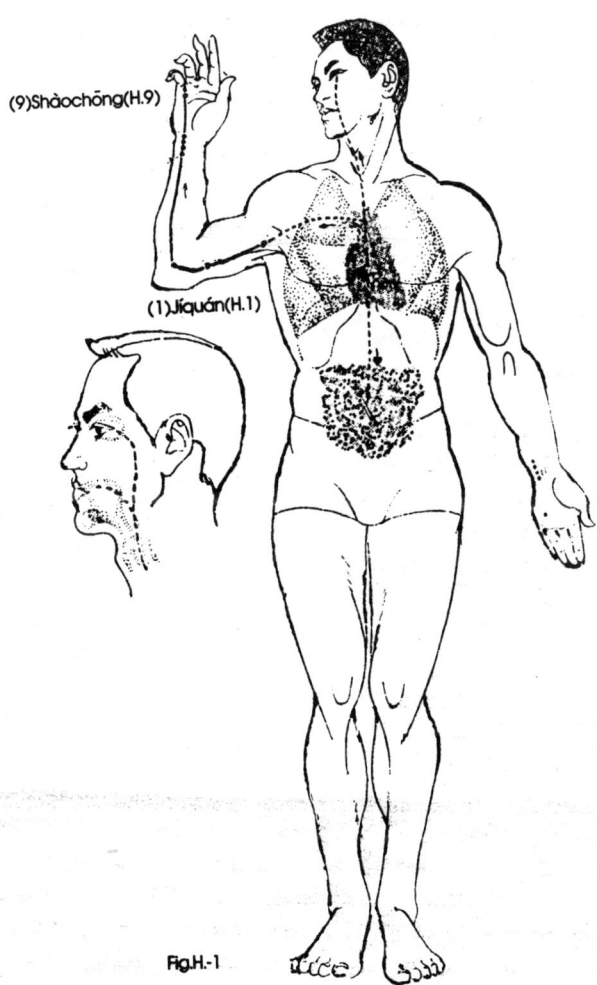

Fig.H.-1

The Heart Miridian of Hand-shàoyīn

Requirements:

While practicing, concentrate on regulating the mind, the respiration and the physical strength. Regulating the mind means making the mind quiet and relaxed; regulating the respiration means paying attention to the rhythm of the respiration; regulating the physical strength means moving gently. The meridian goes from the chest to the hand. The Qi in the meridian should link with the eyes and open onto the tongue. There are altogether nine points. Remember the starting and ending points (Jiquan H.1 and Shaochong H.9), as well as Shaohai (H. 3) and Shengmen (H. 7). Acupuncturists and Qigong masters should remember all the points.

Location of the important points: (Fig.Sp.-2)

1. Jiquan: In the center of the axilla, on the medial side of the axillary artery.

3. Shaohai: When the elbow is flexed, the point is at the medial end of the transverse cubital crease in the depression in front of the medial epicondylus of the humerus.

7. Shengmen: On the transverse crease of the wrist, in the articular region between the pisiform bone and the ulna, in the depression on the radial side of the tendon of flexor carpi ulnaris muscle.

9. Shaochong: On the radial side of the little finger, about 0.1 cun behind the corner of the nail.

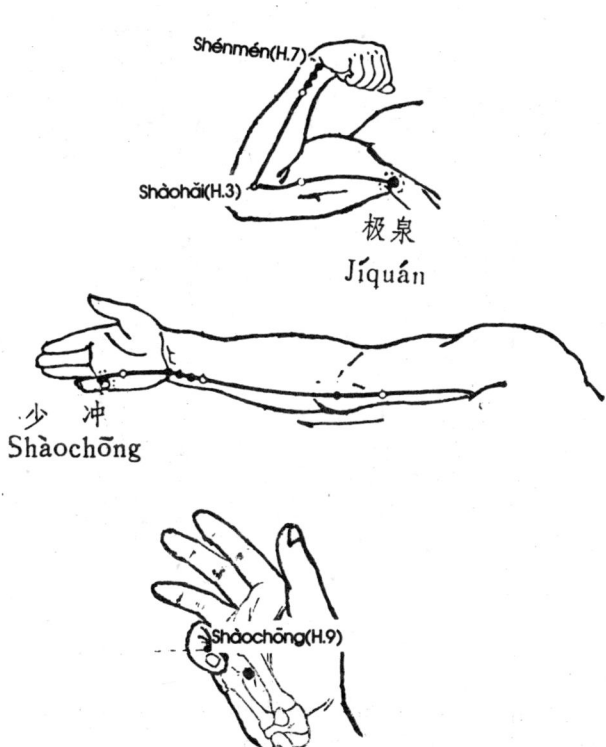

Fig.H.-2 The Heart Miridian of Hand-shàoyīn

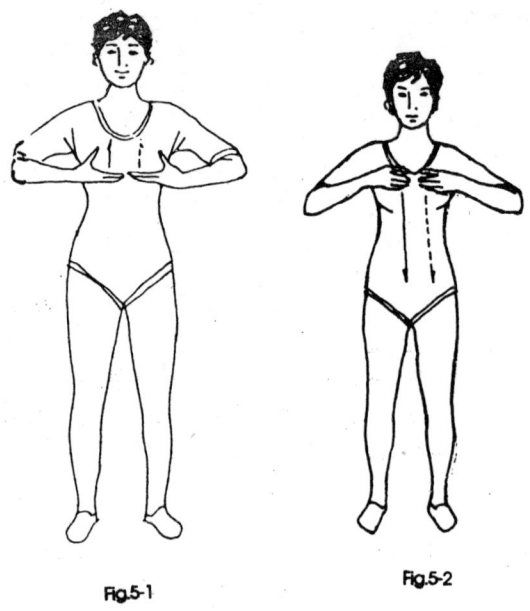

Fig.5-1 Fig.5-2

Instructions:

1. Start from the heart and go down to connect with the small intestine (Figs. 5-1, 5-2, 5-3).

While inhaling raise the hands upward slightly, with the palms facing up. While exhaling turn the palms face down and drop them slowly to the position of the small intestine.

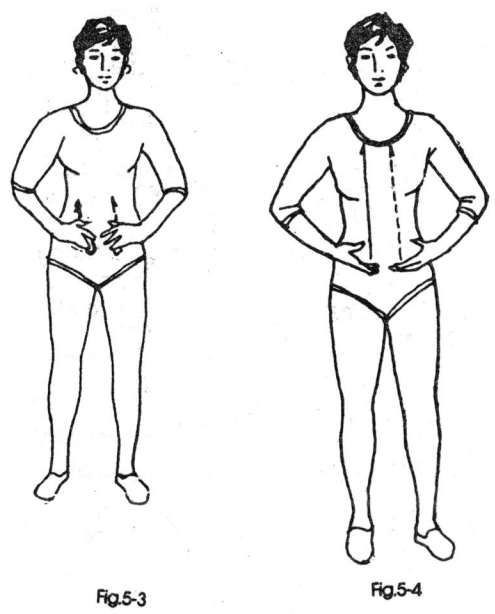

Fig.5-3   Fig.5-4

2. Go to the heart, up to the eyes, into the brain and through the ears (Figs. 5-4, 5-5).

While inhaling slowly, turn the palms upward and raise the hands slowly to the heart. Continue moving upward alongside the esophagus, until the Qi conncets with the eyes, enters the brain and goes through the ears. Massage the eyes with the palms six times. Breathe normally.

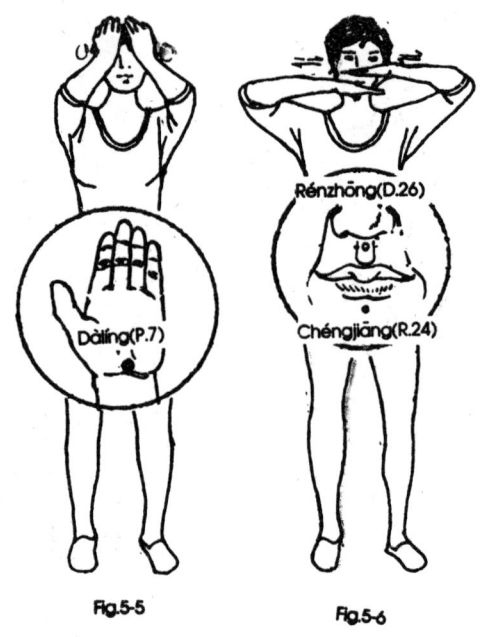

Fig.5-5   Fig.5-6

3. Opening into the mouth and spreading onto the tip of the tongue (Fig. 5-6).

Place the index fingers along the upper and lower lips. Rub back and forth six times. The tip of the tongue should be resting against the roof of the mouth behind the front teeth. Visualize the Qi spreading onto the tip of the tongue. Breathe normally.

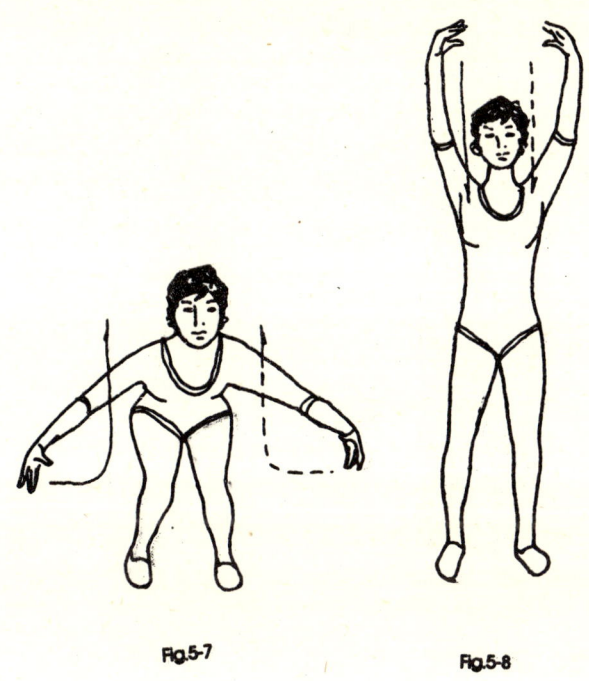

Fig.5-7   Fig.5-8

4. Hold the Qi and pour it into the heart (Figs. 5-7, 5-8, 5-9).
Bend the knees and hold the Qi.
Straighten the body and lift the arms over the head.
Pour the Qi into the heart.

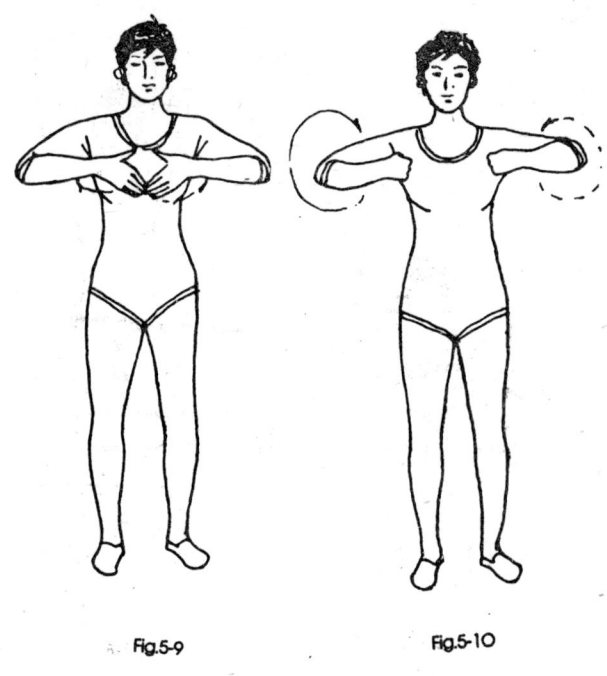

Fig.5-9   Fig.5-10

5. Go laterally to the axillae and rotate the arms three times (Fig. 5-10).

Move the hands to the axillae (Jiquan H. 1). Rotate the arms from front to back three times. Breathe normally.

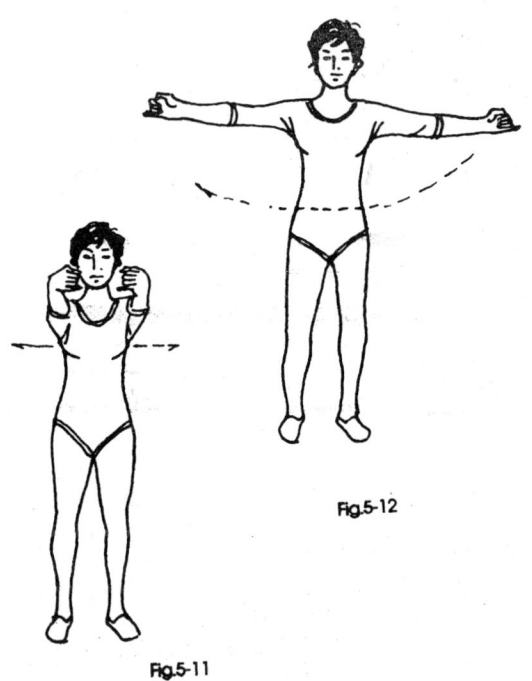

Fig.5-12

Fig.5-11

6. Stretch the arms and extend the little fingers (Figs. 5-11, 5-12).

While inhaling deeply, stretch the arms to the sides simultaneously bending all the fingers except the little fingers. Have the mind go to the medial tip of the little fingers by passing through the chest and along the route.

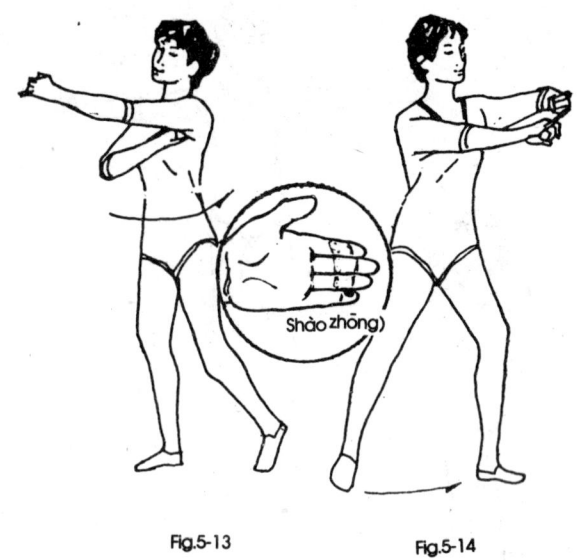

Fig.5-13 Fig.5-14

7. Move the Qi along the left meridian (Fig. 5-13, 5-14).

Turn the trunk completely to the right, step one step to the left with the left foot. Bend the right arm and put the little finger on the Jiquan (H. 1) in the axilla. While exhaling slowly, turn the trunk gradually to the left. At the same time the right hand should move the Qi along the meridian, and the points should be recited silently.

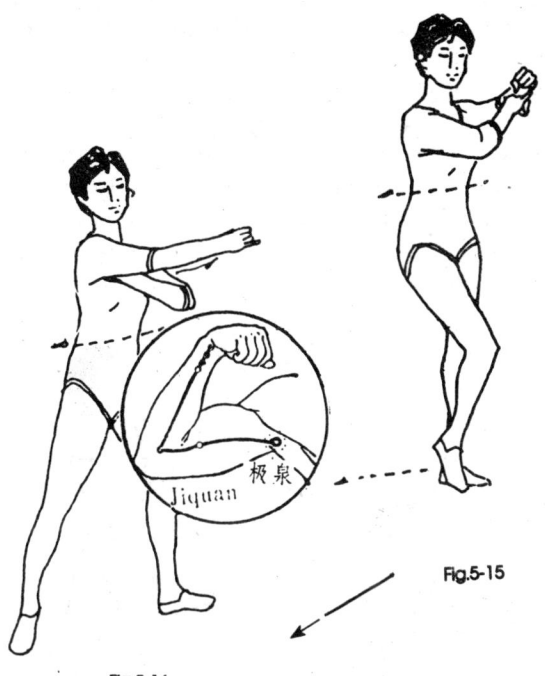

Fig.5-15

Fig.5-16

8. Breathe in and turn to the right (Fig. 5-15).

When the Qi hads been moved to Shaochong (H. 9), bring the right foot together with the left foot. While inhaling deeply, raise the arms and turn the trunk to the right. The weight shifts to the right foot. The left foot takes a step to the left, and the right little finger returns to Jiquan. While exhaling start moving the Qi along the left meridian. Move the Qi along the left meridian twice.

9. Move the Qi along the right meridian (Figs. 5-16, 5-17).

While inhaling, bring the right foot together with the left foot. Shift the weight to the left foot. Turn the trunk to the left completely and take a step with the right foot to the right. Put the left little finger on the Jiquan point. While exhaling slowly, turn the trunk to the right. At the same time the left hand should move the Qi along the meridian and the points should be read silently. Move the Qi along the right meridian and the points twice.

Fig.5-17

Fig.5-18

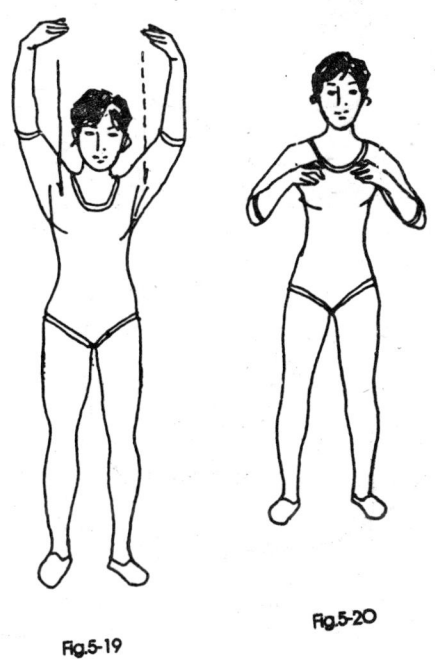

Fig.5-19 Fig.5-20

10. Raise the arms and move the Qi downward (Figs. 5-18, 5-19).

When the left little finger gets to the medial side of the right little finger, move the left foot to keep the feet at shoulders width. While inhaling slowly raise the arms over the head. While exhaling move the arms downward.

11. Turn the fingers to connects with the next meridian (Figs. 5-20, 5-21).

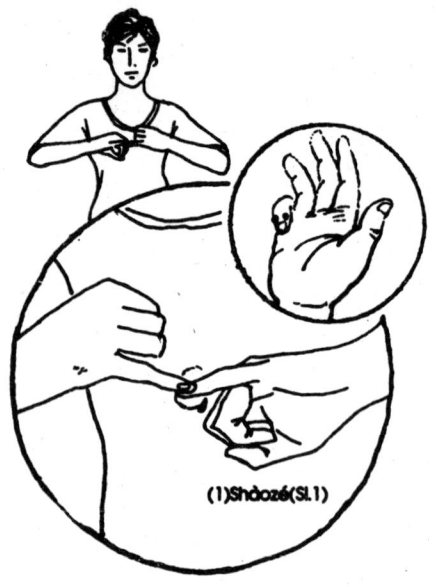

(1)Shàozé(SI.1)

Fig.5-21

When the hands go to the front of the chest, touch the left Shaochong with the right little finger. Turn the left wrist clockwise and the right little finger can touch the left Shaoze (SI. 1). Repeat this same action with the right Shaochong.

VI. The Small Intestine Meridian of the Hand-Taiyang

(Flow route):

The small Intestine Meridian of the Hand-Taiyang originates from the outer side of the tip of the little finger (Shaoze, SI. 1). From there it ascends along the posterior border of the lateral aspect of the arm to the shoulder joint. Circling around the scapula or shoulder blade, it meets the Dazhui point. There the meridian forks into a shallow and a deep branch. The deep one descends to the lung to connect with the heart. Passing through the diaphragm, it enters the small intestine. The Qi goes to Xiajuxu (S. 39). The shallow one ascends to the neck from the supraclavicular fossa and beyond to the cheek (Quanliao, SI. 18). At the outer canthi and Tinggong (SI. 19), it enters the ear. A branch emerges at Quanliao and runs upward to the inner canthi (Jingming, B. 1) where it links with the Urinary Bladder Meridian of the Foot-Taiyang.

Indications: (Fig. SI.-1)

Pain in the lateral aspects of the arms, sore throat, chronic diarrhea, mild disorders of cervical vertebrae, blurring of vision, and pain in the neck and the scapular region.

Requirements:

While practicing, concentrate on regulating the respiration and the force of the actions. While the hands move the Qi to Jianzhen point (SI. 9), straighten and bend the weight-bearing leg following an "M" route.

The meridian flows from the hand to the head. There

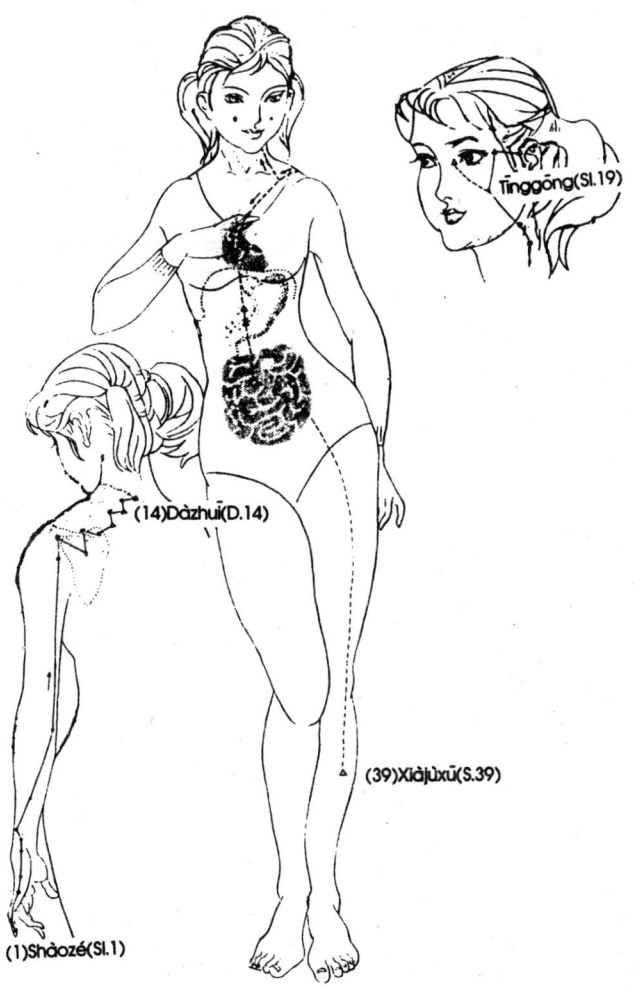

Fig.SI.-1 The Small Intestine Meridian of Hand-Tàiyáng

are altogether 19 points. Remember the starting point Shaoze and the ending point Tinggong, as well as Yanglao (SI. 6), and Jianzhen (SI. 9) and Quanliao (SI. 18). Acupuncturists and Qigong masters should remember all the points.

Location of the important points: (Fig. SI.-2)

1. Shaoze: On the ulnar side of the little finger, about 0.1 cun behind the corner of the nail.

6. Yanglao: Dorsal to the head of the ulna. When the palm faces the chest, the point is in the bony cleft on the radial side of the styloid process of the ulna.

8. Xiaohai: Between the olecranon of the ulna and the medial epicondylus of the humerus.

9. Jianzhen: Behind and below the shoulder joint, when the arm is adducted, the point is 1 cun above the posterior end of the axillary fold.

10. Naoshu: When the arm is adducted, the point is directly above Jianzhen, in the depression below and to the side of the scapular spine.

11. Tianzhong: In the infrascapular fossa, at the junction of the upper and middle third of the distance between the lower border of the scapular spine and the inferior angle of the scapula.

17. Tianrong: Behind the angle of the mandible, in the depression on the front edge of the sternocleidomastoideus muscle.

18. Quanliao: Directly below the outer canthus, in the depression on the lower border of Zygoma.

19. Tinggong: Between the tragus and the mandibular joint, where a depression is formed when the mouth is slightly open.

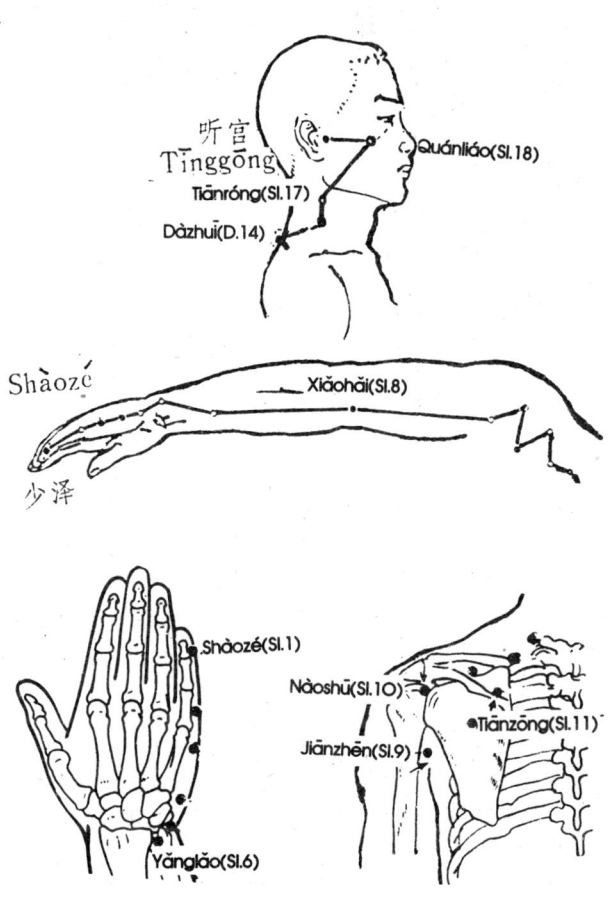

Fig.SI.-2 The Small Intestine Meridian of Hand-Tàiyáng

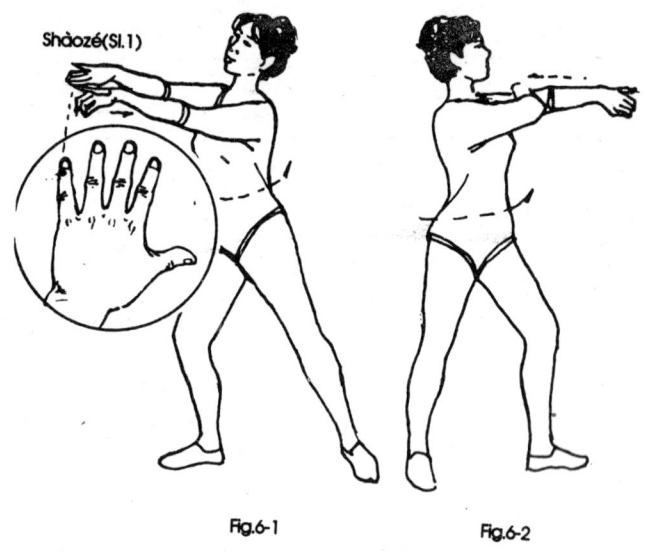

Fig.6-1   Fig.6-2

Instructions:

1. Turn the body and stretch the arms out to the right (Fig. 6-1).

Turn the trunk and the right foot 90 degrees to the right. At the same time stretch the arms out to the right. Put the right index finger on the left Shaoze. The weight is on the right foot. Take a step backward with the left foot. Breathe normally.

2. Turn to the left to move the Qi of the left side. (Fig. 6-2).

Gradually turn the trunk, the right foot 135 and the left foot 90 degrees to the left while moving the Qi along the meridian.

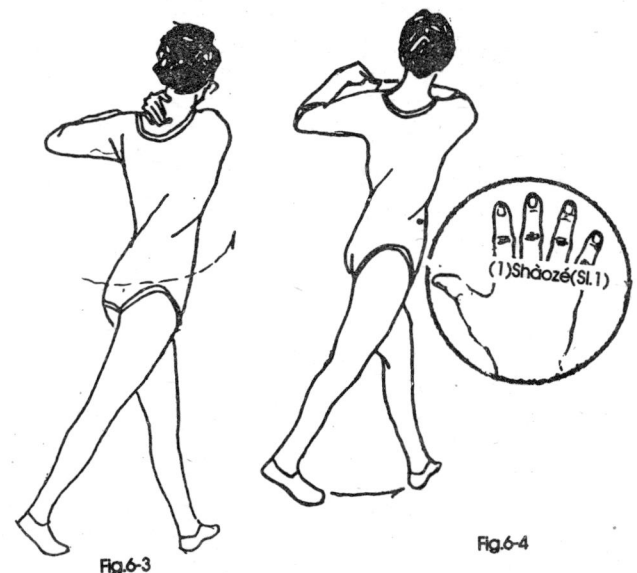

Fig.6-3 Fig.6-4

Notes:
While exhaling, move the Qi from the starting point to the elbow. While inhaling, move the Qi from the elbow to Dazhui. When the Qi has been moved to Jianzhen (SI. 9), straighten and bend the right leg up and down twice making an "M" in the air.

3. Meet Dazhui (Fig. 6-3).

When the Qi has been moved to Dazhui, bend the left arm. Put the left index finger on the right Shaoze. At that time the inhalation should be finished.

4. Turn to the left and take a step forward with the right foot (Fig. 6-4).

Turn the left foot 45 and the trunk to the left. Take a step forward with the right foot. Exhale during this action.

Fig.6-5

Fig.6-6

5. Turn to the right to move the Qi of the right side (Fig. 6-5).

While stretching the arms out forward, turn the trunk and the right foot 45 degrees to the right. At the same time the left index finger should move the Qi upward along the route. When the Qi has been moved to Jianzhen, straighten and bend the left leg up and down twice making an "M" in the air.

Notes:

See the notes in action (2).

Move the Qi twice on each side.

6. Turn the body and bring the fingers together (Figs. 6-6, 6-7).

While exhaling turn to the right the right foot 90

Fig.6-7   Fig.6-8

degrees and the body. Move the left foot so as to keep the feet at shoulder width. While inhaling raise the arms from the back and baring the fingers together.

7. Touch Dazhui (Figs. 6-8, 6-9).

While exhaling drop the hands slowly to touch Dazhui.

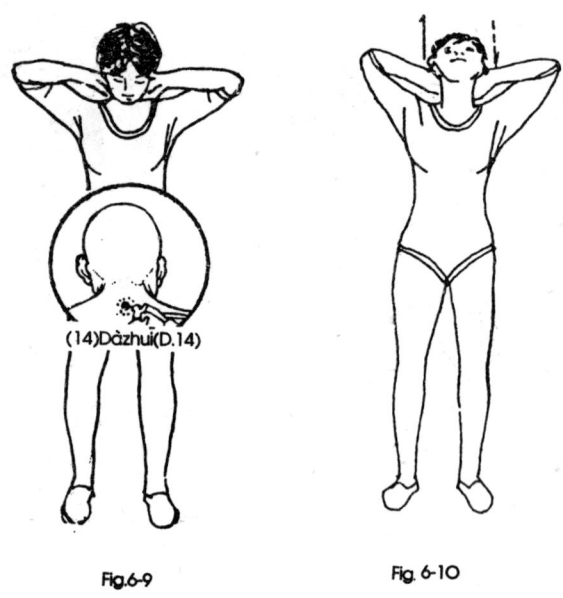

Fig.6-9 Fig. 6-10

8. Move Dazhui, breathe normally (Figs. 6-9, 6-10, 6-11, 6-12, 6-13, 6-14).

Nod and raise the head six times.

Turn the trunk and the limbs to the left and right six times. Turn Dazhui to the sides six times (see actions (8), (9), (10), (11), and (12) in the Large Intesstine Meridian).

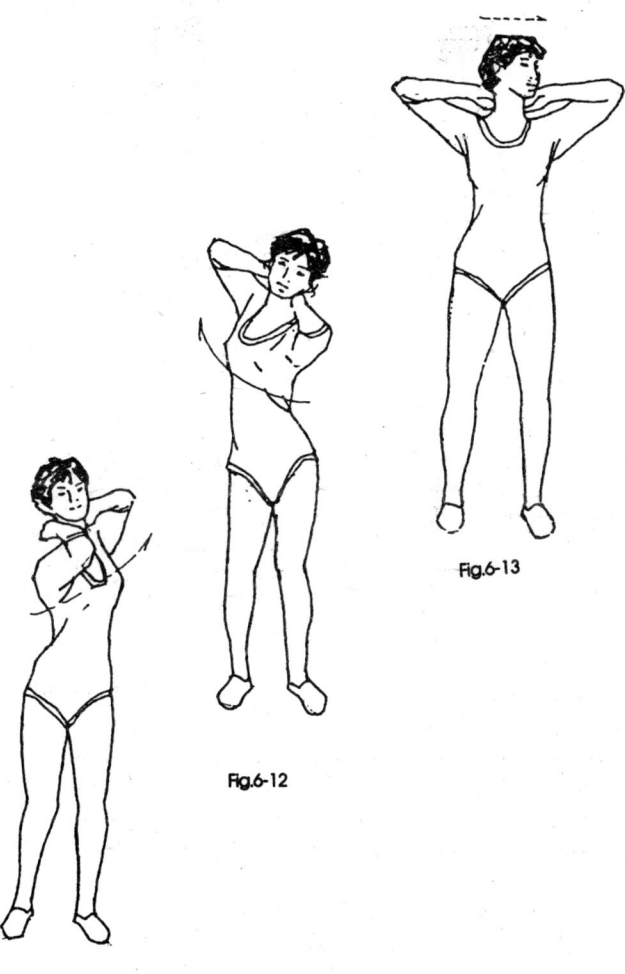

Fig.6-11

Fig.6-12

Fig.6-13

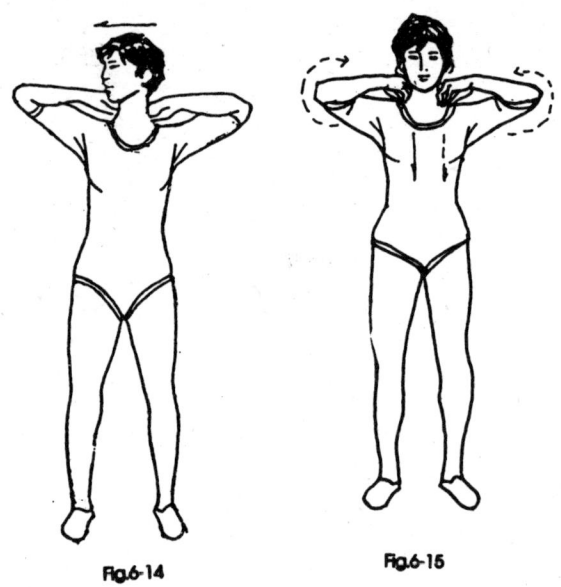

Fig.6-14 Fig.6-15

9. Go to the supraclavicular fossa, rotate the arms three times (Fig. 6-15).

Move the hands to the supraclavicular fossa and rotate the arms from the front to the back three times. Breathe normally. Be aware of the two branches that emerge at this point. First move the Qi in the internal one.

10. Descend to connect with the heart (Fig. 6-15).

While exhaling drop the hands to the chest and then to the heart. Pause and then, while inhaling, have the mind connect with the heart.

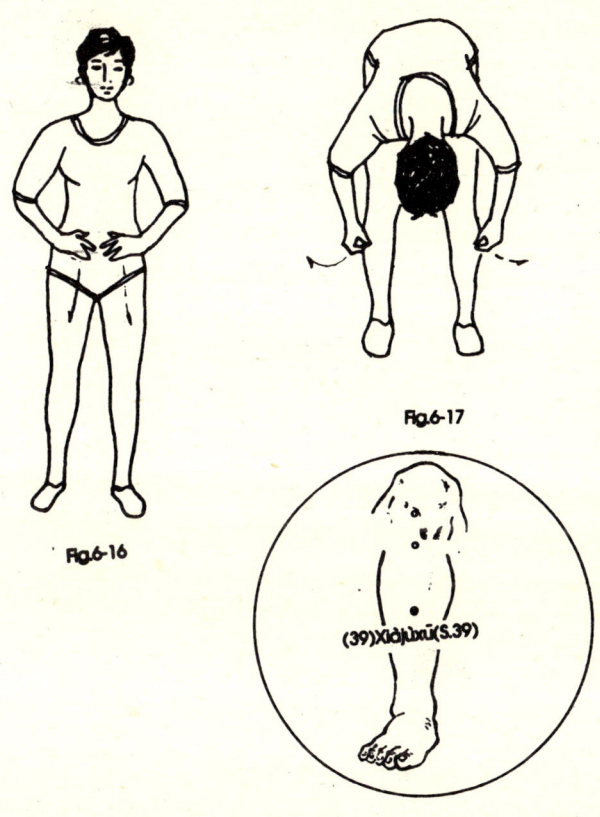

Fig.6-16

Fig.6-17

(39)Xiàjùxū(S.39)

Fig.6-18

11. Pass through the diaphragm and enter the small intestine (Fig. 6-16).

While exhaling drop the hands from the heart. Passing through the diaphragm, the Qi enters the small intestine. Pause and concentrate on it while inhaling.

12. Go downward to meet Xiajuxu (Figs. 6-17, 6-18).

While exhaling slowly, bend forward and move the hands to Xiajuxu (S. 39).

13. Bend the knees and hold the Qi (Figs. 6-19, 6-20)

Inhale as you slowly straighten the body, and lift the arms over the head.

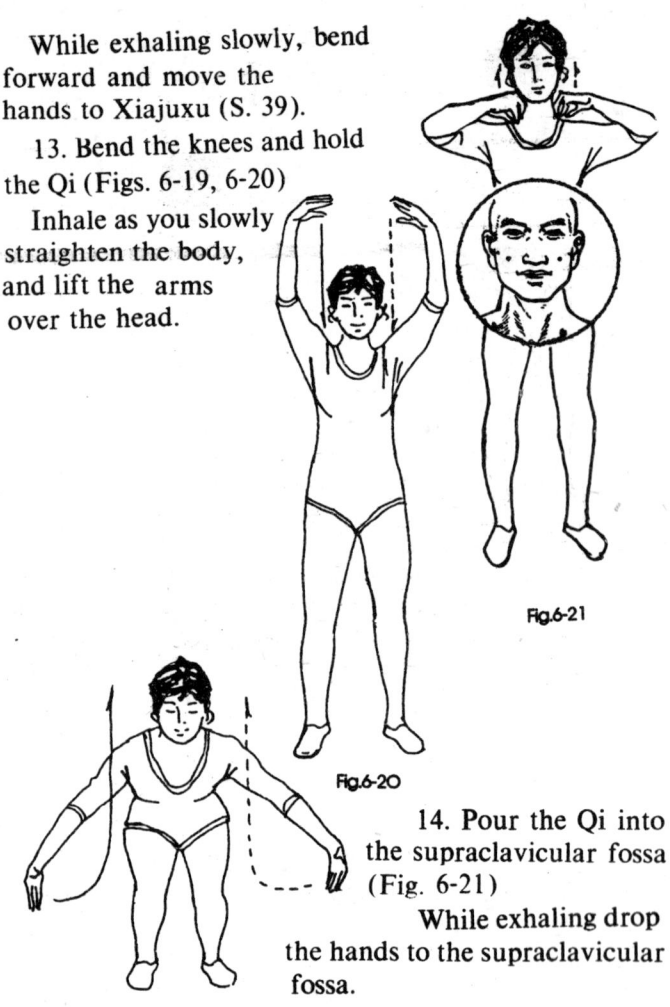

Fig.6-21

Fig.6-20

Fig.6-19

14. Pour the Qi into the supraclavicular fossa (Fig. 6-21)

While exhaling drop the hands to the supraclavicular fossa.

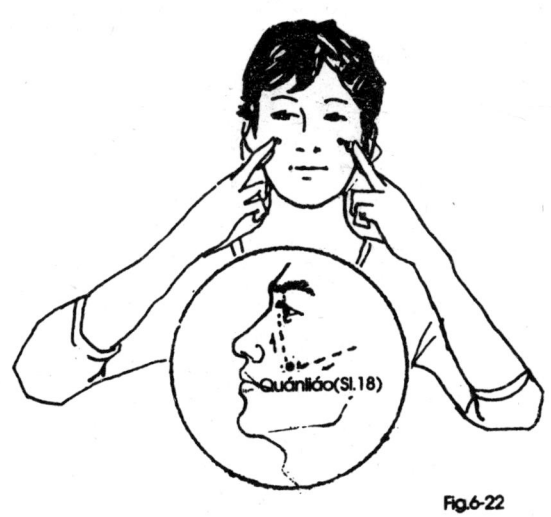

Fig.6-22

15. Ascend along the superficial route and massage Tinggong (SI. 19) (Figs. 6-22, 6-23).

The hands ascend along the route to Quanliao (SI. 18) and Tinggong (SI. 19) where the Qi enters the ears.

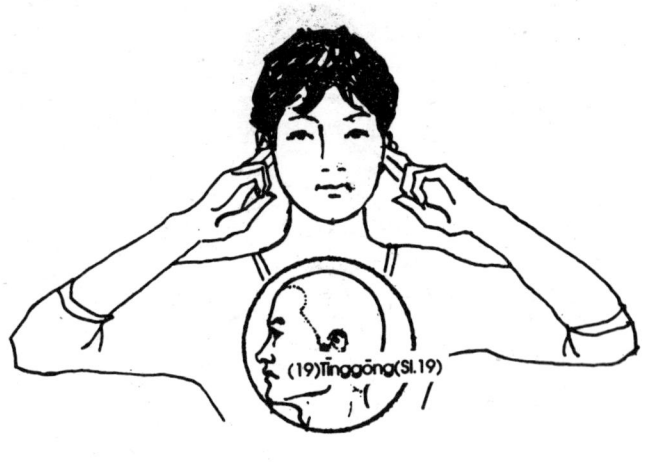

Fig.6-23

Massage Tinggong six times. Go back to Quanliao and reach Jingming (B. 1) where the Qi connects with the Qi in the Urinary Bladder Meridian of the Foot-Taiyang.

VII. The Bladder Meridian of the Foot-Taiyang

Flow route: (Fig. B.-1)

The Bladder Meridian of the Foot-Taiyang starts from the inner canthus (Jingming B. 1). Ascending to the forehead and passing the medial end of the eyebrow (Zanzhu, B. 2), it joints the Du Meridian at the vertex (top of the head). Proceeding downward, it reaches the Tianzhu point (B. 10). From there, the meridian branches into two. The internal one meets Dazhui (D. 14). The two branches (one is 2.5 cun and the other is 3 cun away from the vertebral column) run downward alongside the vertebral column. At the kidney region, one branch enters the body cavity to connect with the kidneys and join its pertaining organ. Descending from the kidney region, this branch meets the other branch in the popliteal fossa (behind the knees) (Weizhong, B. 40). Continuing downward along the posterior border of the lateral aspect of the tibia, the meridian reaches the lateral side of the tip of the little toe (Zhiyin, B. 67). From Zhiyin, the end point, it goes to the bottom of the foot, where it links with the Kidney Meridian of the Foot-Shaoyin.

Indications:

As the meridian goes from the head to the foot, and the internal organs (Zang-fu organs) have their Shu points in the back region, this is the most important meridian for regulating the functions of the viscera. Points on the meridian are also used to treat pain in the head, neck, lumbar, and sacral region of the back and the joints in the lower limbs. The meridian has the particular function of invigorating the kidneys, strengthening Yang, and regulating the function of the

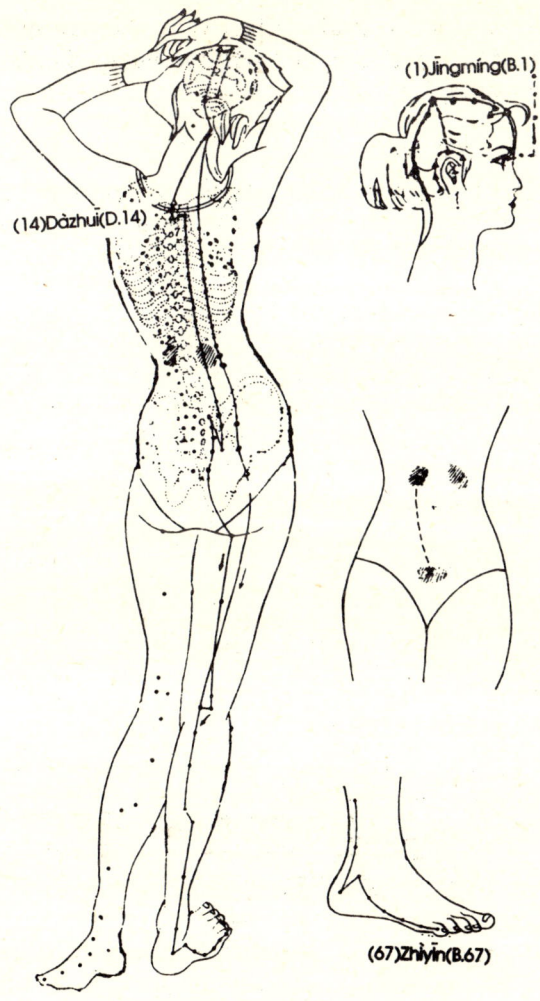

Fig.B.-1 The Bladder Meridian of Foot-TàiYáng

urinary bladder. It is also effective in the treatment of impotence, premature ejaculation, hemorrhoids and hypogonadia.

Requirements:

While practicing, concentrate on massaging the points on the head. Contract the muscles of the anus and genitals and clench the teeth while lifting the kidney Qi.

Be clearly aware of the route of the meridian: two branches emerge at Tianzhu (B. 10) where the internal one goes to meet Dazhui (D. 14); then the two branches meet together in the popliteal fossa (behind the knees). Remember the starting point and the ending points (Jingming and Zhiyin), in addition to Zanzhu (B. 2) , Tianzhu (B. 10), Shenshu (B. 23). Weizhong (B. 40), and Zhishi (B. 52). You should know the Shu points in the back region. Acupuncturists and Qigong masters should remember all the points and go through them silently while moving the Qi.

Location of the important points: (Fig. B.-2)

1. Jingming: Just 0.1 cun above the inner canthus.

2. Zanzhú: On the medial extremity of the eyebrow, or on the supra-orbital notch.

10. Tianzhú: About 1.3 cun to the side of Yamen (D. 15), behind the back hairline, on the side of the trapezius muscle.

23. Shènshū: About 1.5 cun to the side of the lower border of the spinous process of the second lumbar vertebra.

40. Wěizhōng: Mid-point of the transverse crease of

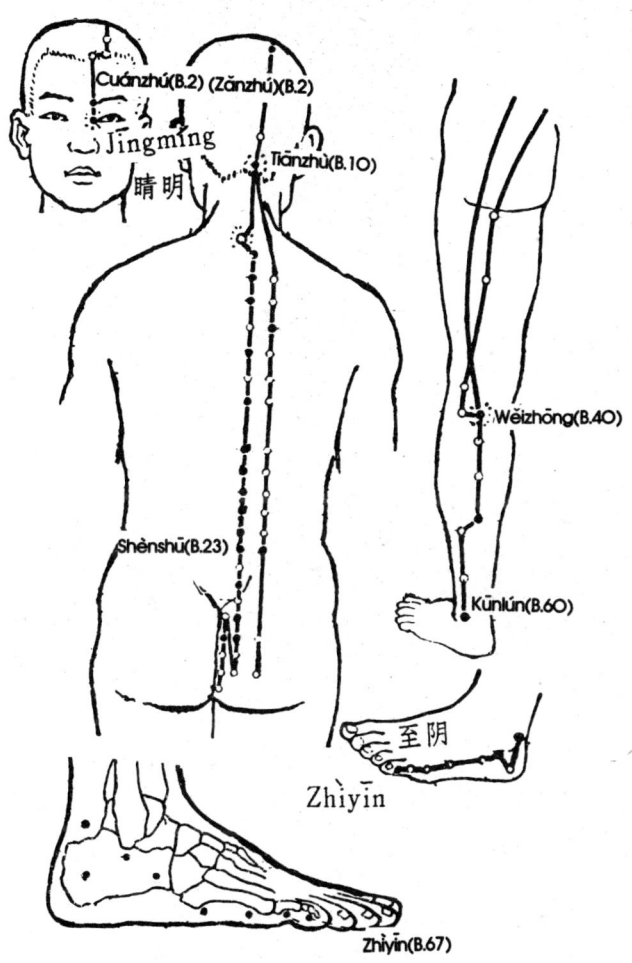

Fig.B.-2   The Bladder Meridian of Foot-TàiYáng

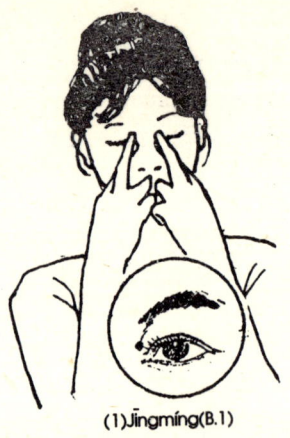

(1)Jīngmíng(B.1)

Fig.7-1

the popliteal fossa.

60. Kūnlún: In the depression between the external malleolus and tendo calcaneus.

67. Zhìyīn: On the lateral side of the small toe, about 0.1 cun behind the corner of the nail.

Fig.7-2

Instructions:

1. Massage Jingming and Cuanzhu to have bright eyes and a clear mind (Figs. 7-1, 7-2).

Massage Jingming six times. Then massage Zanzhu six times. While massaging, you should feel slight soreness.

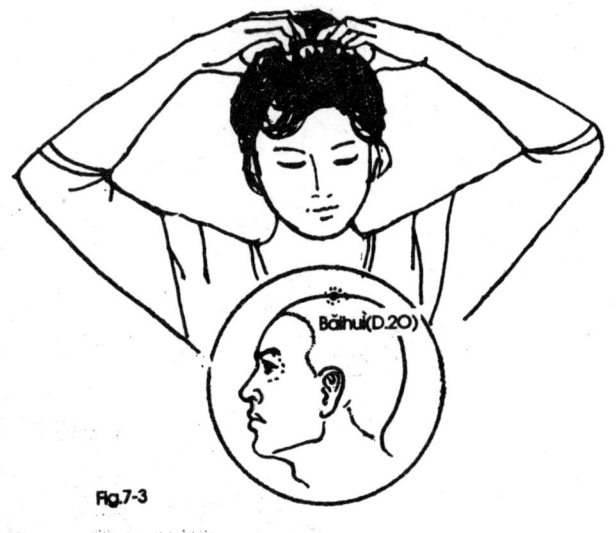

Fig. 7-3

2. Go to the vertex, enter the brain and connect with the ears (Fig. 7-3).

The hands go upward along the meridian to the vertex of the head. Use the middle fingers to massage Baihui (D. 20) six times. At the same time, visualize the Qi entering the brain and connecting with the ears.

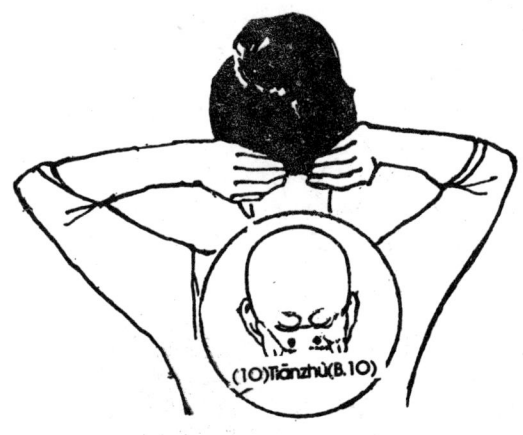

Fig. 7-4

3. Massage Tianzhu (B. 10) to relax the tendons and clear the meridian passage (Fig. 7-4).

Massage Tianzhu six times. You should get a slight sensation of soreness and distension. This is to relax the tendons and clear the meridian passage.

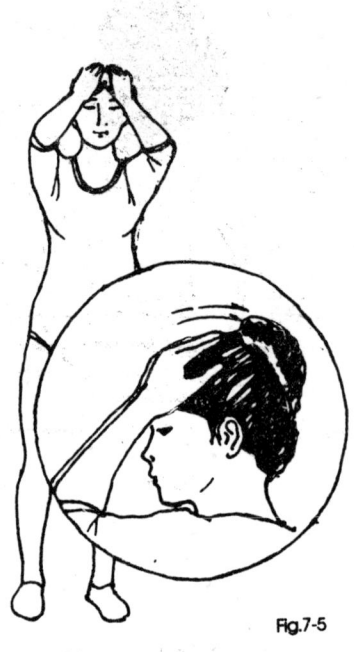

Fig.7-5

4. Massage the skull and rotate Dazhui (Figs. 7-5, 7-6).

Use the palms to massage the paths on the skull from Zanzhu to Tianzhu six times. At Tianzhu, the two

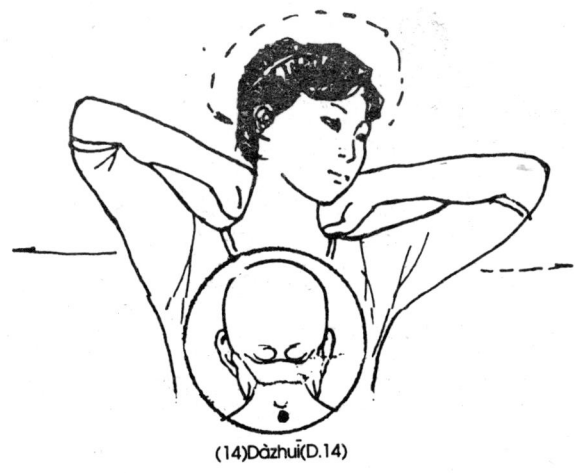

(14)Dàzhui(D.14)

Fig.7-6

branches emerge. The internal one goes to meet Dazhui. Rotate Dazhui clockwise six times and counterclockwise six times.

Fig.7-7

Fig.7-8

5. Stretch the arms out wide and put the palms face down (Fig. 7-7).

While inhaling stretch the arms out wide and put the palms face down. While exhaling, gradually bend over and turn the palms face up.

6. Bend the arms, put the hands on the back, straighten the trunk (Fig. 7-8).

Bend the arms and put the backs of the hands on the back as high as possible. Put the thumbs and index fingers on the two branches. While inhaling, straighten the body slowly and move the fingers downward along the routes.

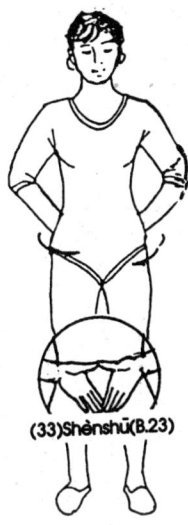

Fig. 7-9

7. Connect with the kidneys and lift the kidney Qi (Fig. 7-9).

When the fingers reach Shenshu (B. 23) and Zhishi (B. 52), the Qi connects with the kidneys. At that time, tense the muscles of the abdomen, contract the muscles around the genitals and anus and clench the teeth. Do this three times. Breathe normally.

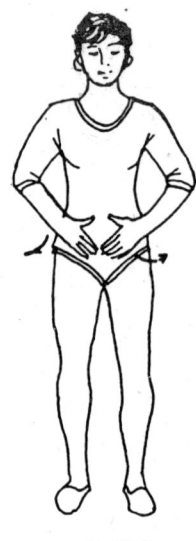

Fig.7-10

8. Enter the urinary bladder and lift the kidney (Fig. 7-10).

Move the hands from the kidney region to the urinary bladder region where the Qi enters the urinary bladder. Again, tense the muscles of the abdomen, contract the muscles of the genitals and anus and clench the teeth. Do this three times. Breathe normally.

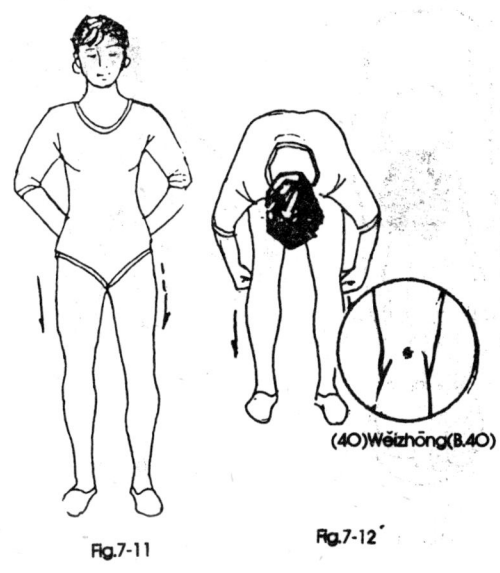

Fig.7-11   Fig.7-12   (40)Weizhong(B.40)

9. Go downward along the route to Zhiyin (B. 67) (Figs. 7-11, 7-12, 7-13).

The hands then return to the kidneys and move downward along the routes to the popliteal fossa (behind the knees) (Weizhong, B. 40) where the two branches become one. From there the hands move the Qi along the route to the ending point, Zhiyin.

Notes:
While moving the Qi exhale and bend over slowly.

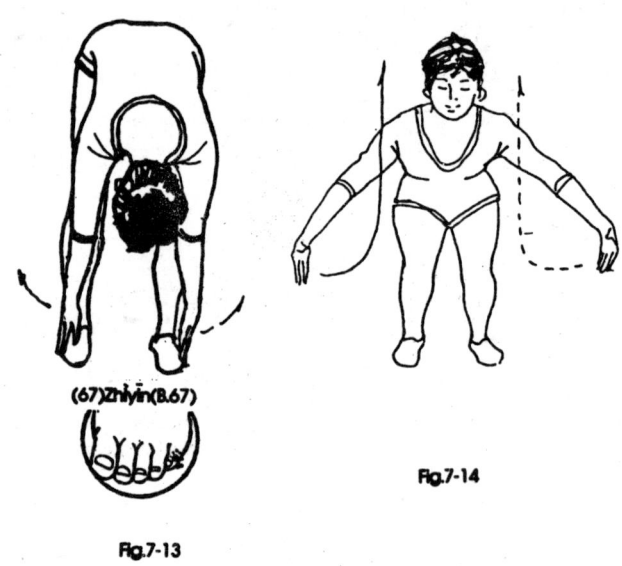

Fig.7-13

Fig.7-14

10. Bend the knees and hold the Qi (Figs. 7-14, 7-15). Straighten the body and lift the arms over the head.

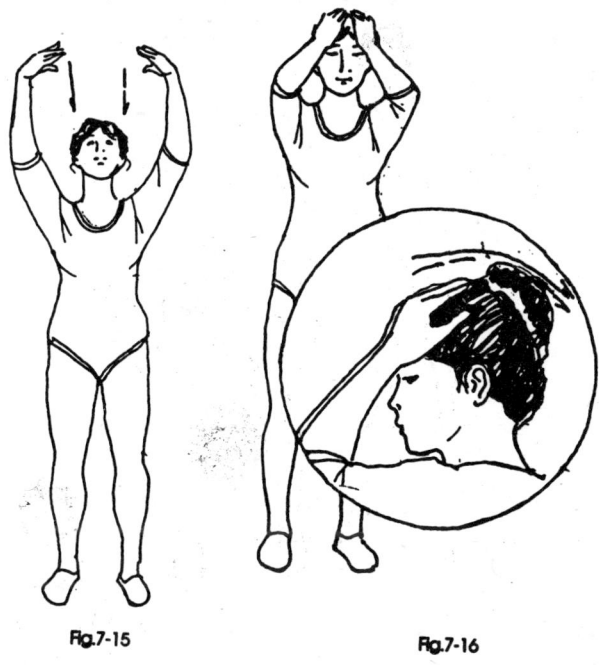

Fig.7-15   Fig.7-16

11. Repeat actions (4), (5), (6), (7), (8), (9). (Figs. 7-16, 7-17, 7-18, 7-19, 7-20).

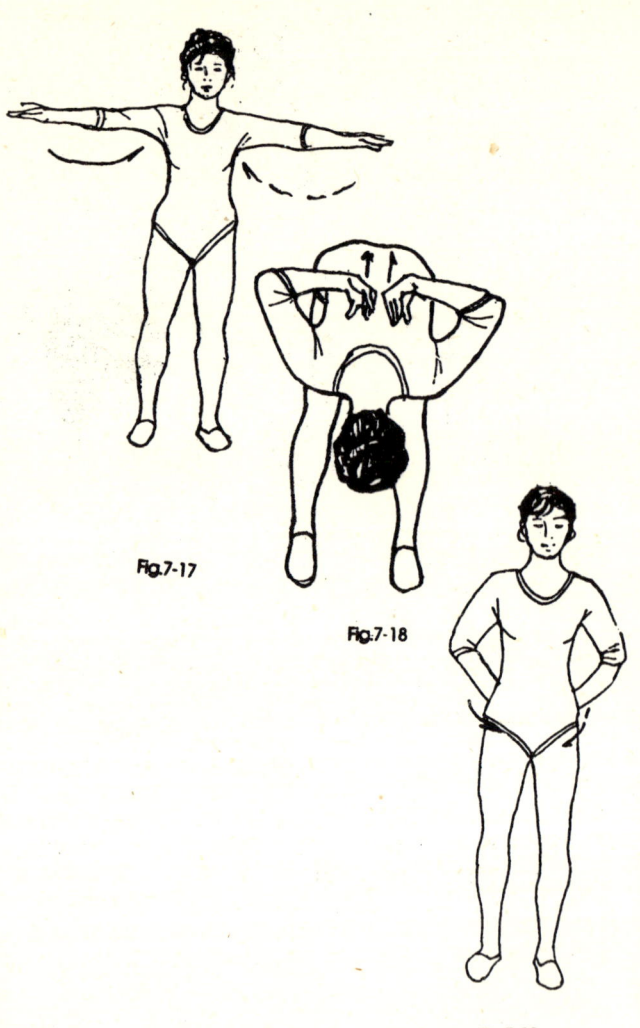

Fig.7-17

Fig.7-18

Fig.7-19

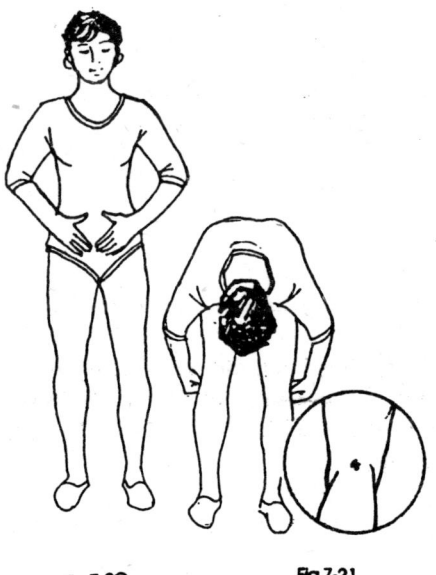

Fig.7-20　　　　Fig.7-21

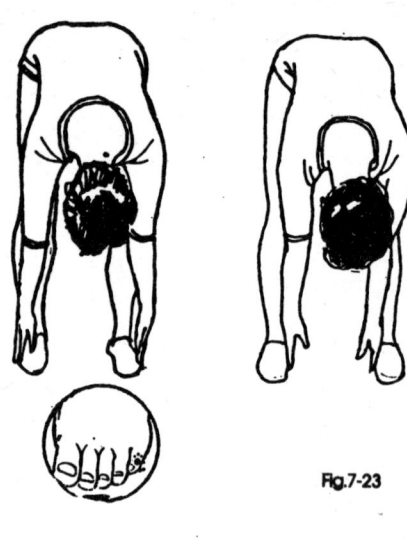

Fig.7-22

Fig.7-23

12. Go to the bottoms of the feet (Figs. 7-21, 7-22, 7-23).

When the Qi has been moved to Zhiyin, visualize the Qi reaching the bottoms of the feet, (Yongquan, K. 1) where it links with the Kidney Meridian of the Foot-Shaoyin.

VIII. The Kidney Meridian of the Foot-Shaoyin

Flow route: (Fig. K.-1)

The Kidney Meridian of the Foot-Shaoyin starts from the interior aspect of the small toe and runs obliquely to the sole (Yongquan, K. 1). Emerging from the lower part of the protruding part of the navicular bone in the pelvic area, it goes around the medial ankle. Then it ascends along the posterior border of the medical aspect of the leg to Huiyin (R. 1) by passing Yingu (K. 10). Winding around the genitals, it goes upward along a line 0.5 cun away from the mid-line of the body to Youmen (K. 21). Then it proceeds upward along a line now 2 cun away from the mid-line to Shufu (K. 27). The internal branch emerging from Huiyin goes back to wind around the anus. Passing Changqiang (D. 1), it goes further upward along the vertebral column. At the Mingmen point (D. 4), it enters the kidneys and connects with the urinary bladder. From the kidneys, ascending along the lateral abdomen, it passes the diaphragm and enters the lungs, runs along the throat and terminates at the root of the tongue. The Qi opens into the ears and spreads over the root of the tongue. A branch springs form each lung, joins the heart and flows into the chest to link with the Pericardium Meridian of the Hand-Jueyin.

Indications:

Abnormal rise in vital energy, asthma, sore throat, palpitations, irritability, visual failure, deafness and tinnitus, pain and fullness in the chest and hypochondrial region, feverish sensation in the soles of the feet, lumbago, and sexual disorders, such as impotence, premature ejaculation and prostatitis.

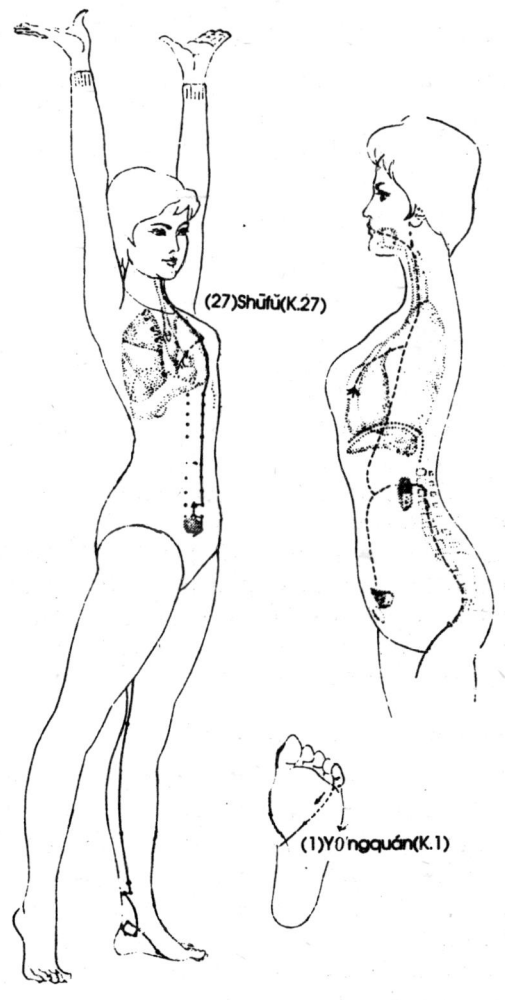

Fig.K.-1 The kidney Meridian of Foot-Shàoyīn

Requirements:

Concentrate on moving the Qi along the route and on controlling the center of gravity in order to keep balance. The meridian goes from the foot to the chest.

Keypoints:

1. As it ascends, the meridian circles the medial ankle.

2. To reach the Huiyin point, the meridian winds around the genitals before it ascends to the abdomen.

3. Proceeding from the Huiyin point, the internal branch winds around the anus before it goes upward along the vertebral column.

4. At Mingmen (D. 4), it enters the kidneys and connects with the urinary bladder.

5. The Qi opens into the ears and spreads over the root of the tongue.

There are altogether 27 points. Remember the starting point Yongquan and the ending point Shufu, as well as Taixi (K. 3), Zhaohai (K. 6) and Zhubin (K. 9). Acupuncturists and Qigong masters should remember all the points.

Location of the important points: (Fig.K-20)

1. Yǒngquán: In the depression appearing on the sole when the foot is in plantar flection, approximately at the junction of the front and middle thirds of the sole.

3. Tàixī: In the depression between the medial malleolus and tendo calcaneus, level with the tip of the medial malleolus.

6. Zhàohǎi: One cun below the medial malleolus.

9. Zhùbīn: On the line drawn from Taixi to Yingu, at the lower end of the gastrocnemius muscle, about 5

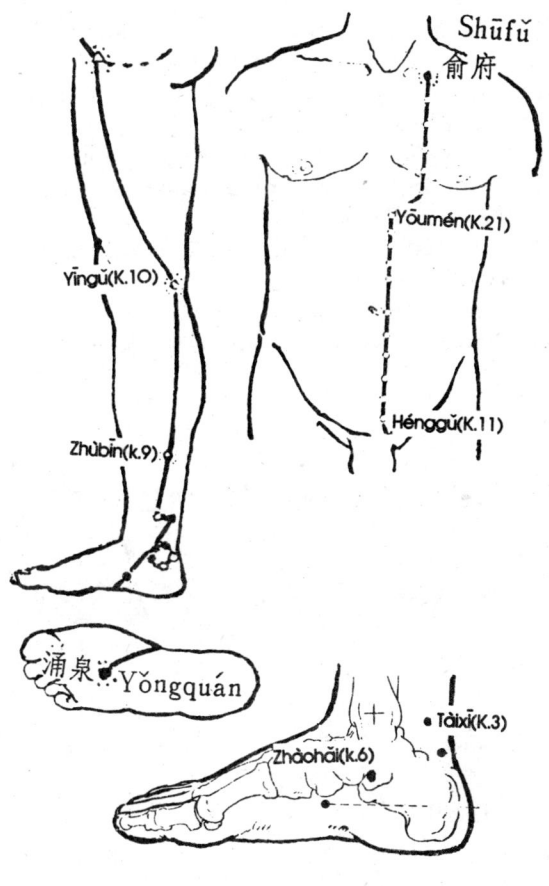

Fig.K.-2   The kidney Meridian of Foot-Shàoyīn

cun above Taixi.

10. Yīngŭ: On the medial side of the popliteal fossa, level with Weizhong, between the tendons of the semitendinosus and semimembranosus muscles when the knee is flexed.

11. Hénggŭ: Five cun below the umbilicus, on the superior border of the symphysis pubis, 0.5 cun to the side of Qugu (R. 2).

21. Yòumén: Six cun above the umbilicus, 0.5 cun to the side of Juque (R. 14).

27. Shūfŭ: In the depression on the lower border of the clavicle, 2 cun to the side of the Ren Meridian.

Instructions:

1. Turn the body to the left and move the Qi along

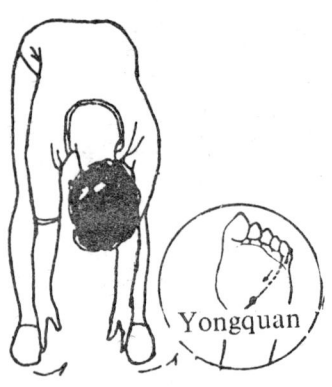

Fig.8-1

Fig.8-2

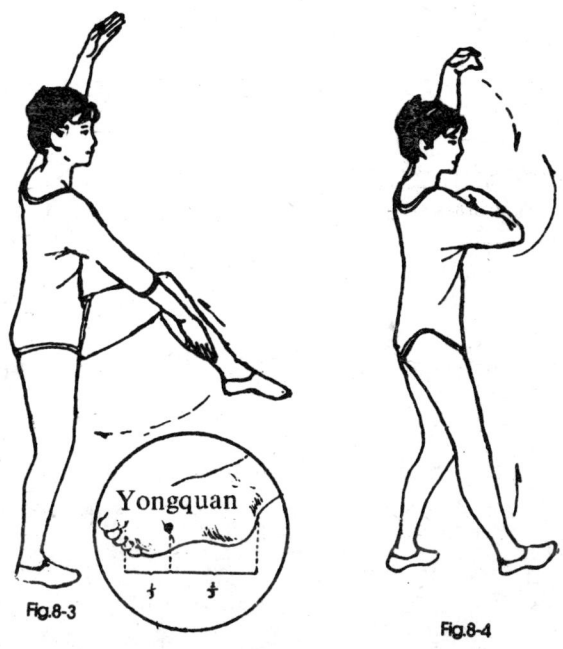

Fig.8-3 Fig.8-4

the route of the left side (Figs. 8-1, 8-2, 8-3).

Turn the right foot 45 degrees and the left foot 90 degrees to the left. Slowly straighten the body, raise the left arm and leg and stretch the right arm to the left foot. Concentrate on the Yongquan point. While inhaling move the Qi upward along the route.

Notes:

The hand should circle the medial ankle.
2. Reach Huiyin and ascend to Shufu (Fig. 8-4).

As the right hand ascends to Huiyin, the raised left foot takes a step backward. Continue to move the Qi

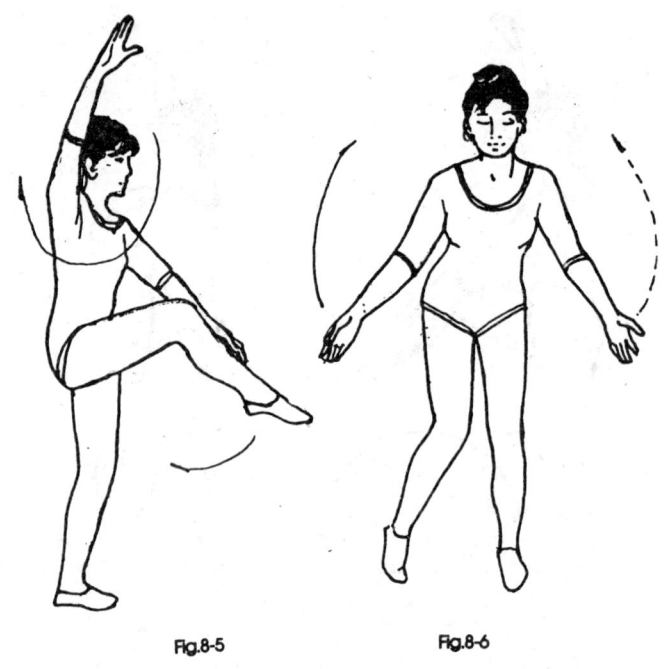

Fig.8-5 Fig.8-6

upward to Youmen (K. 21). Start exhaling.

3. Move the Qi along the right side. (Fig. 8-5).

While exhaling drop the left arm and raise the right arm and leg. Stretch the left arm to the Yongquan and concentrate on it. While inhaling move the Qi upward along the route. When the left hand reaches Huiyin, take a step backward with the raised right foot. Continue moving the Qi on the above Youmen. Start exhaling. Move the Qi twice along the route each side.

Fig.8-7   Fig.8-8

4. Turn the body and raise the arms (Figs. 8-6, 8-7).

Turn the left foot 90 degrees and the body to the right. Move the right foot so as to keep the feet at shoulders' width. While inhaling, gradually raise the arms.

5. Move the bilateral Qi (Fig. 8-8).

While exhaling bend over and touch the feet. Concentrate on Yongquan. While inhaling move the Qi upward to Huiyin, as the body is slowly straightened.

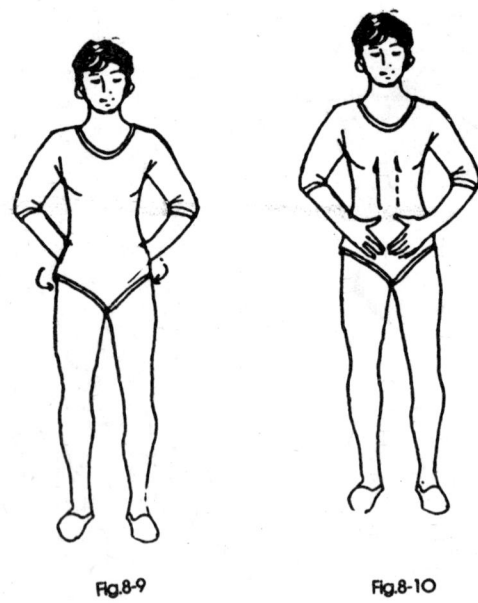

Fig.8-9 Fig.8-10

6. Enter the kidneys and lift the kidney Qi (Fig. 8-9).

While exhaling move the hands to the back. Concentrate on Huiyin. Then in the mind wind around the anus to Changqiang (D. 1). Ascending along the vertebral column, it reaches Mingmen, where it enters the kidneys. Put the back of the hands on the kidneys. While breathing normally, contract the muscles around the genitals and anus and clench the teeth. Do this three times.

7. Connect with the urinary bladder (Fig. 8-10).

The hands descend from the kidneys to go backwards to the lower abdomen and connect with the urinary bladder. Concentrate on the urinary bladder. Put the

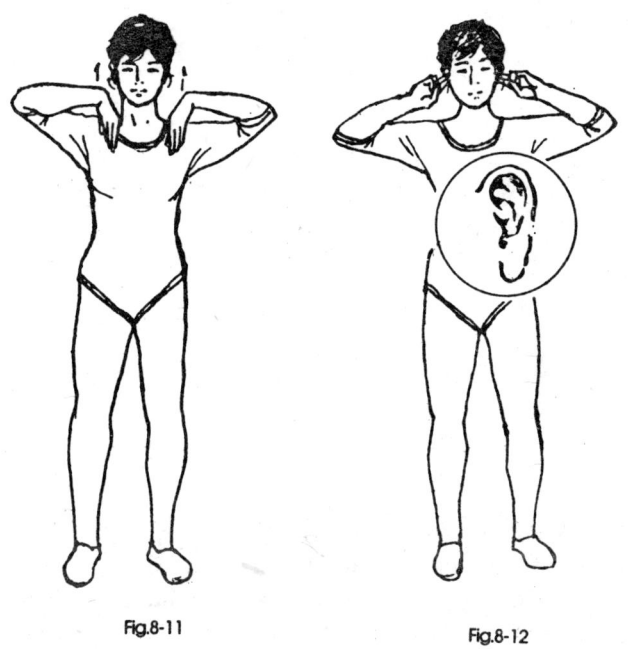

Fig.8-11 Fig.8-12

palms on the abdomen. While breathing normally, tense the muscles of the abdomen, contract the muscles around the genitals and anus and clench the teeth. Do this three times.

8. Pass through the diaphragm (Fig. 8-11).

While inhaling move the hands upward along the lateral abdomen, let the Qi pass through the diaphragm, enter the lungs and run along the throat and the root of the tongue.

9. Open into the ears (Fig. 8-12).

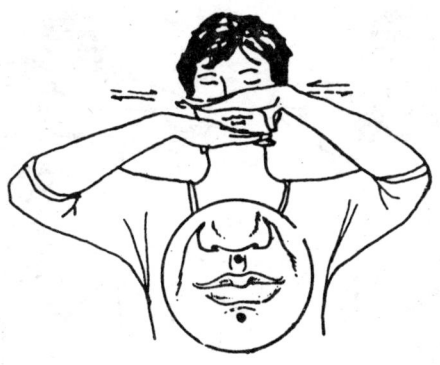

Fig.8-13

The hands ascend along the routes. The Qi goes through the ears. Put the middle fingers on the index fingers. Massage the tragi (the cartilaginous projections in front of the ears) with the fingers six times. Breathe normally.

10. The Qi curves around the mouth and spreads onto the root of the tongue (Fig. 8-13).

Place the index fingers along the upper and lower lips. Rub back and forth six times. Visualize the Qi spreading on to the root of the tongue.

Fig.8-14

Fig.8-15

11. Bend the knees and hold the Qi (Figs. 8-14, 8-15, 8-16, 8-17, 8-18).

Straighten the body and lift the arms over the head. Move the bilateral Qi. Repeat the actions (6) (7).

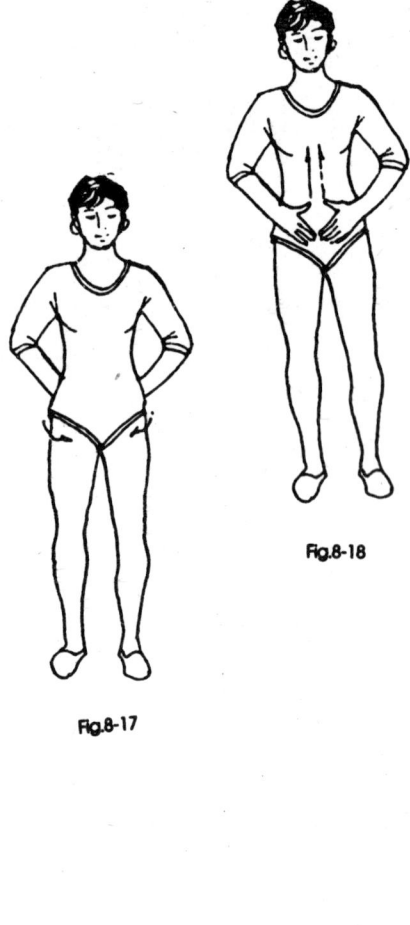

Fig.8-18

Fig.8-17

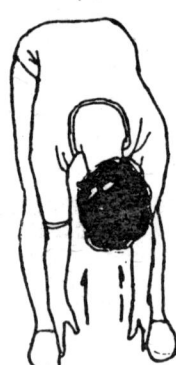

Fig.8-16

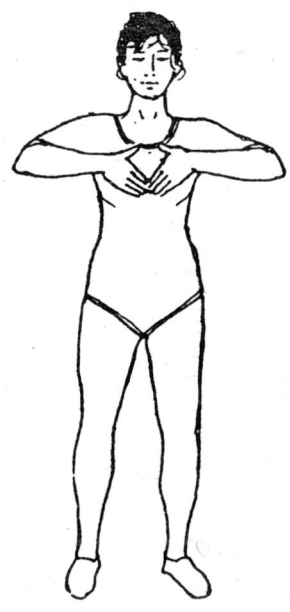

Fig.8-19

12. Ascend to the chest and link with the Pericardium (Fig. 8-19).

While inhaling move the hands upward along the lateral abdomen to the lungs. A branch emerges from the lungs, links with the heart, and flows into the chest, where it links with the Pericardium Meridian of the Hand-Jueyin.

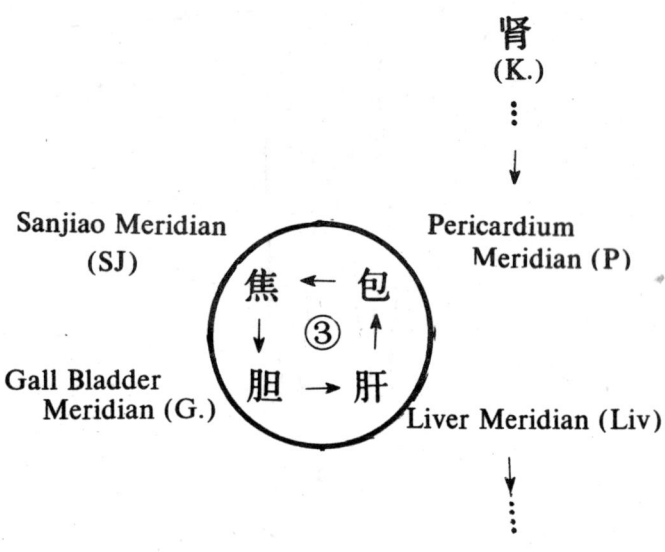

IX. The Pericardium Meridian of the Hand-Jueyin

Flow route: (Fig. P.-1)

The Pericardium Meridian of the Hand-Jueyin starts from the chest. Beginning there, it enters the pericardium sac surrounding the heart, its pertaining organ. Then it descends through the diaphragm to the abdomen connecting successively with the upper, middle and lower jiao. Then as it returns to the pericardium, it runs alongside the esophagus. The meridian goes up until it links with the eyes and enters the brain. The superficial meridian arises from the chest and run inside the chest emerging from the rib region at the Tianchi point (P. 1), 1 cun to the side of the nipple and ascending to the axilla. Running downward along the mid-line of the medial aspect of the arm, it reaches the tip of the middle finger (Zhongchong, P. 9)

A branch arises from the palm at Laogong (P.8) and runs along the ring finger to its tip to link with the Sanjiao Meridian of the Hand-Shaoyang.

Indications:

Cardiac pain, palpitation, irritability, insomnia, distension of the chest and the hypochondria region, feverish sensation in the palms, neurasthenia and dream-disturbed sleep.

Requirements:

Concentrate on regulating the heart, the respiration, the Qi and the strength. The mind follows the Qi as it is moved along the meridian. Combine the Qi and the strength.

The meridian goes from the chest to the hand

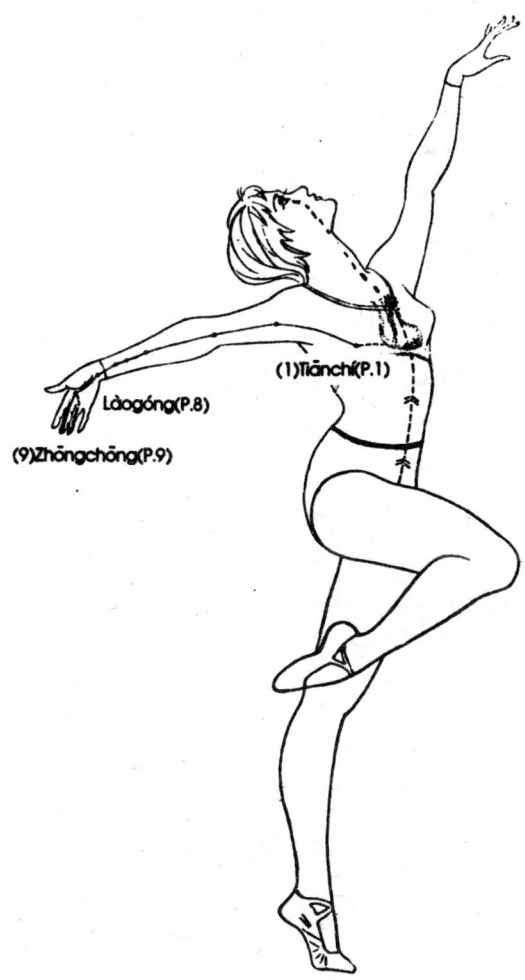

Fig.P.-1 The Pericardium Meridian of Hand-Juéyīn

along the mid-line of the medial aspect of the arm. Remember the starting point Tianchi and the ending point Zhongchong, besides Neiguan (P. 6) and Laogong (P. 8). Be very clear about the two following key points:

1. The meridian ascends from the pericardium to link with the eyes and enter the brain.

2. A branch emerges at Laogong and goes along the medial side of the ring finger. There are altogether nine points. Those who are acupuncturists and Qigong masters should recite all these points while moving the Qi along the meridian.

Location of the important points: (Fig. P.-2)

1. Tiānchí: One cun lateral to the nipple, in the fourth intercostal space.

3. Qūzé: On the transverse cubital crease, at the ulnar side of the biceps brachii tendon.

6. Nèiguān: Two cun above the transverse crease of the wrist, between the palmaris longus and flexor carpi radialis tendons.

7. Dàlíng: In the depression in the middle of the transverse crease of the wrist, between the palmaris longus and flexor carpi radialis tendons.

8. Láogōng: When the hand is placed with the palm upward, the point is between the second and third metacarpal bones, proximal to the metcarpophalangeal joint, on the radial side of the third metacarpal bone.

9. Zhōngchōng: In the center of the tip of the middle finger.

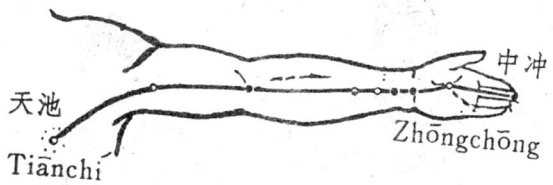
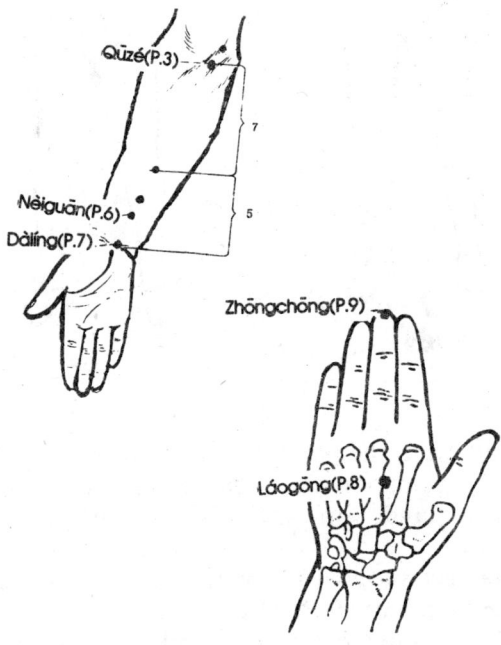

Fig.P.-2 The Pericardium Meridian of Hand-Juéyīn

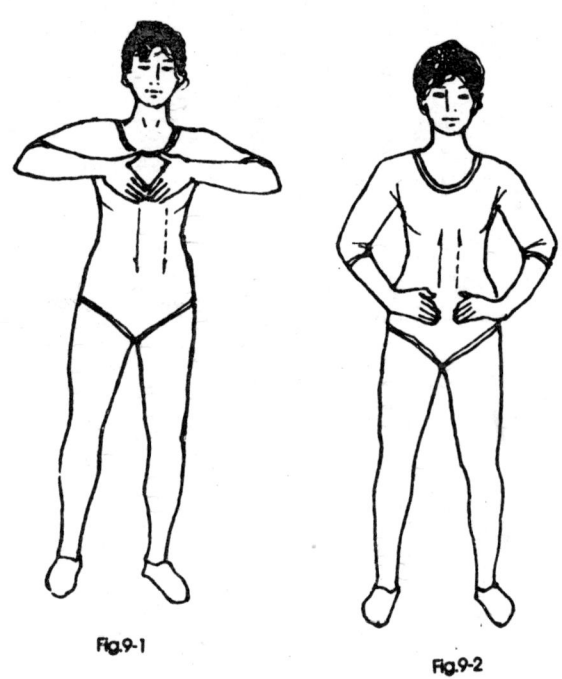

Fig.9-1

Fig.9-2

Instructions:

1. Start from the pericardium (Fig. 9-1).

Put the palms on the pericardium. While inhaling raise the hands upward slightly with the palms facing up.

2. Connect successively with the three jiao and go back to the pericardium (Fig. 9-2).

While exhaling move the hands downward to the abdomen from the chest connecting successively with the upper, middle and lower jiao. While inhaling raise the hands from the lower jiao to the pericardium.

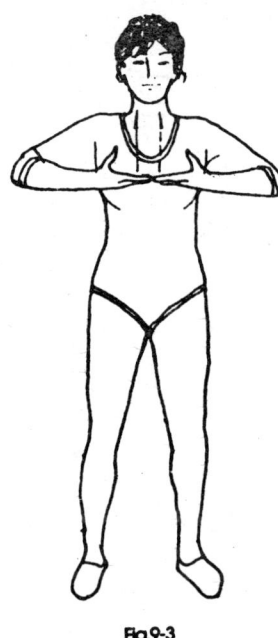

Fig.9-3

3. Run alongside the esophagus to link with the eyes and enter the brain (Fig. 9-3).

While continuing to inhale raise the hands. Let your thoughts trace the length of the esophagus, link with the eyes and enter the brain.

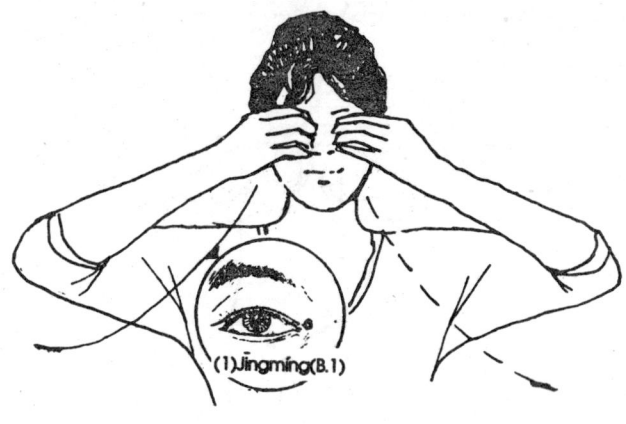

Fig.9-4

4. Massage the eyeballs (Fig. 9-4).

Touch the inner canthi, where the eyelids meet, with the middle fingers. Gently massage the eyeballs six times. Breathe normally.

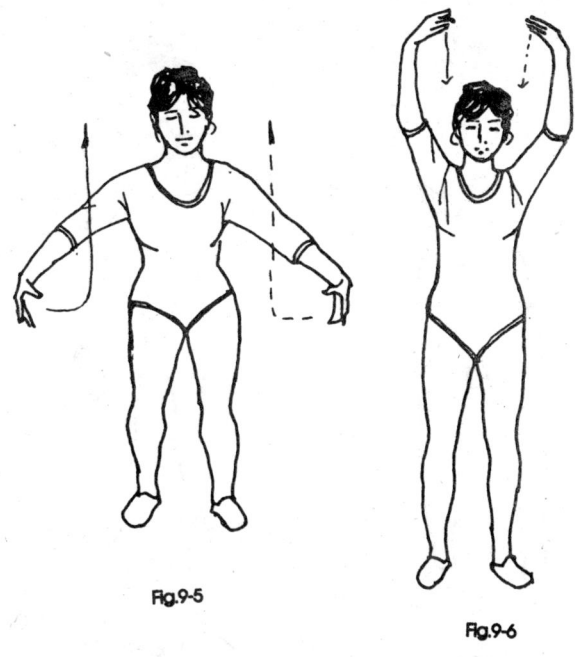

Fig.9-5

Fig.9-6

5. Bend the knees and hold the Qi (Fig. 9-5, 9-6, 9-7). Straighten the body and lift the arms over the head. Pour the Qi into the pericardium.

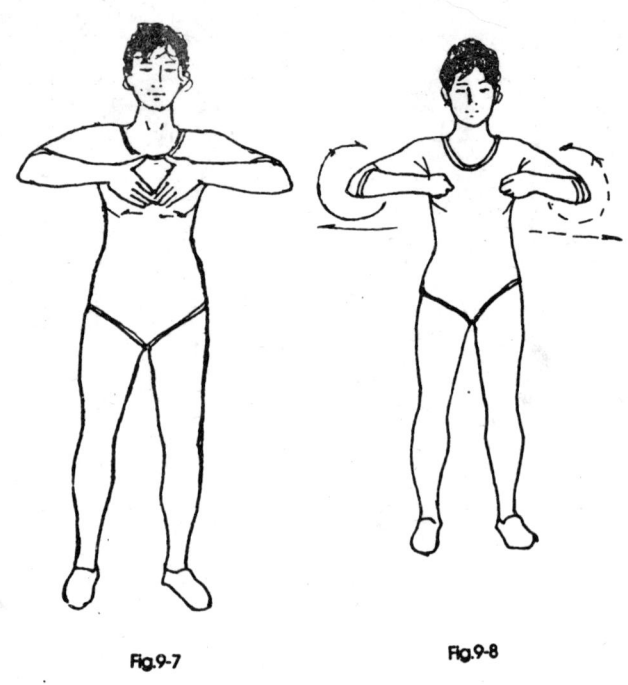

Fig.9-7   Fig.9-8

6. Rotate the arms at Tianchi three times (Fig. 9-8). Move the hands to Tianchi. Here the meridian is superficial. Press the Tianchi points with the middle fingers and rotate the arms three times. Breathe naturally.

Fig.9-9

Fig.9-10

7. Stretch the arms and extend the middle fingers (Fig. 9-9)

While inhaling stretch the arms to the sides, simultaneously bending all the fingers except the middle fingers. The mind runs along the routes to the Zhongchong points.

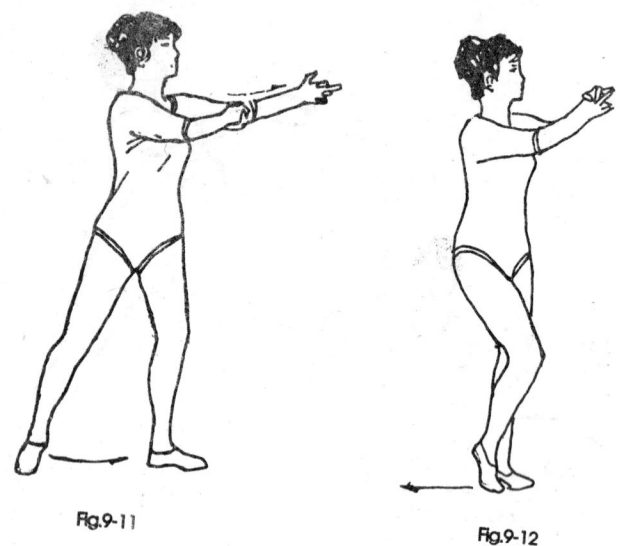

Fig.9-11

Fig.9-12

8. Move the Qi along the left meridian (Figs. 9-10, 9-11, 9-12).

Turn the trunk to the right completely. Put the weight on the right foot. Bend the right arm, put the middle finger on the left Tianchi point, and step one step to the left with the left foot. While exhaling slowly turn the trunk gradually to the left. At the same time the right hand should move the Qi along the left meridian and the points should be read silently. When the Qi has been moved to Zhongchong, bring the right foot together with the left foot. While inhaling raise the arms and turn the trunk to the right. The weight shifts on the right foot. Step one step to the left with the left foot. Put the right middle finger on the left Tianchi point. While exhaling start moving the Qi along the left

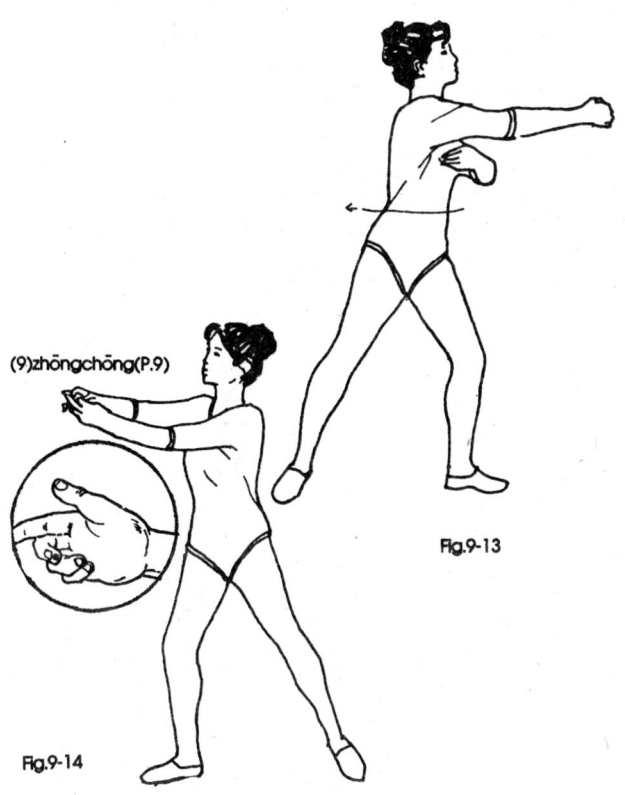

(9) zhōngchōng (P.9)

Fig.9-13

Fig.9-14

meridian again.

(Move the Qi along the left meridian twice.)

9. Move the Qi along the right meridian (Figs. 9-13, 9-14).

While inhaling bring the right foot together with the left foot. Turn the trunk to the left completely and take a step with the right foot to the right. Put the left

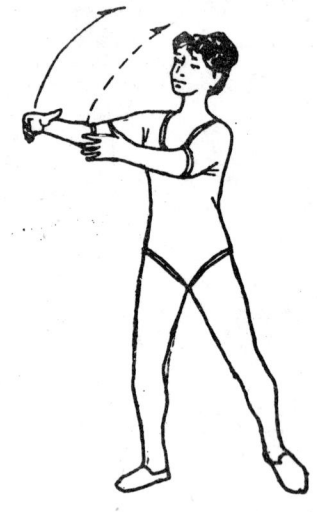

Fig.9-15

middle finger on the right Tianchi point. While exhaling slowly, turn the trunk to the right. At the same time the left hand should move the Qi along the meridian and the points should be read silently.

Move the Qi along the right meridian twice.

10. Move the Qi from Laogong to Guanchong (Figs. 9-15, 9-16, 9-17, 9-18).

While inhaling raise the arms over the head. Move the left foot to keep the feet at shoulders width. While exhaling drop the arms slowly to the front of the chest. Turn the left palm upward. Then with the right middle finger touch the left Laogong. Move the Qi from

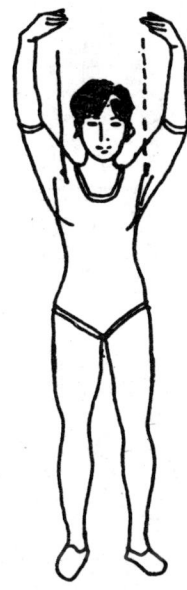

Fig.9-16

Laogong to Guanchong (SJ. 1). After that turn the left palm downward and turn the right palm upward, and the left middle finger should move the Qi from the right Laogong to Guanchong. Guanchong is the linking point that connects the Sanjiao Meridian of the Hand-Shaoyang with the Pericardium Meridian of the Hand-Jueyin.

劳宫
Laogong

Fig.9-17

X. The Sanjiao Meridian of the Hand-Shaoyang

Flow route: (Fig. SJ.-1)

The Sanjiao Meridian of the Hand-Shaoyang starts at the tip of the side of the ring finger (Guanchong) (SJ. 1) and runs upward along the side of the ring finger and the dorsal aspect of the wrist. It passes through the olecranon and along the mid-line of the lateral aspect of the upper arm until it reaches the shoulder region and meets with the Dazhui point (D. 14). Winding over to the supraclavicular fossa, it spreads through the chest, where two branches emerge. The internal branch connects with the pericardium and descends through the diaphragm down to the abdomen and joins its pertaining parts, the upper, middle and lower jiao. The Qi can then go downward to Weiyang (B. 39). The superficial branch starts at the chest. Running upward, it emerges from the supraclavicular fossa. From there it ascends the neck and runs along the posterior border of the ear. At Yifeng it enters the ear and goes to the eye. Then it circles upward and returns to the ear, where it emerges in front. Passing through Ermen (SJ. 21) and Erheliao (SJ. 22), it reaches the lateral end of the eyebrow Sizhukong (SJ. 23). From there, it descends to the outer canthus Tongziliao (G. 1) to link with the Gall Bladder Meridian of the Foot-Shaoyang.

Indications:

Mild deafness, tinnitus, impaired hearing, unilateral headache, eye pain, pain in the shoulders and arms.

Requirements:

Concentrate on regulating the respiration. While

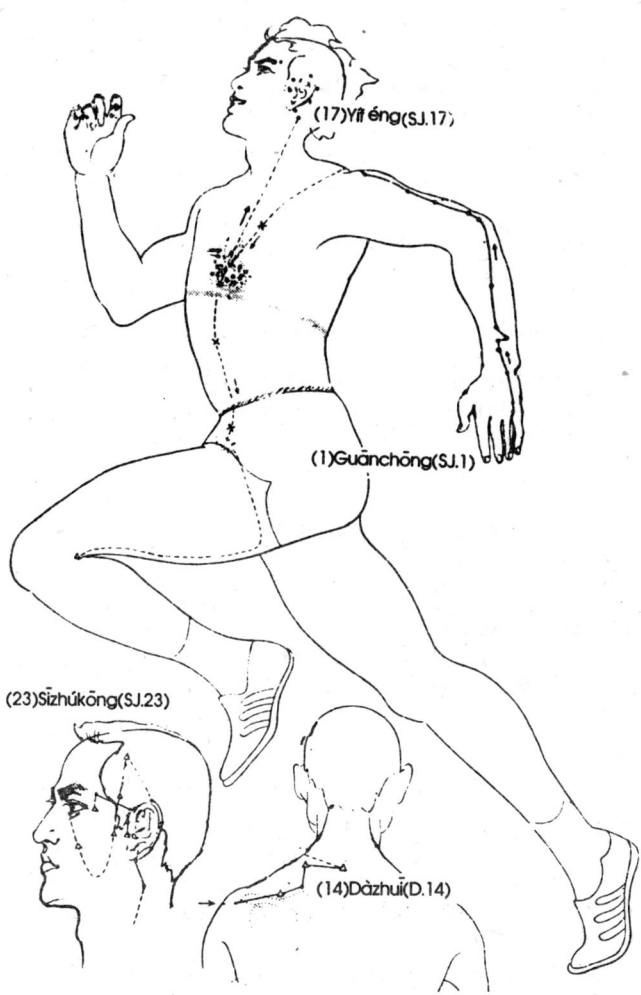

Fig.SJ.-1 The Sānjiāo Meridian of Hand-Shàoyáng

exhaling, move the Qi from the starting point to the elbow. While inhaling, move the Qi from the elbow to Dazhui. The meridian goes from the hand to the head. Remember the starting Guanchong point and the ending Sizhukong point, as well as Waiguan (SJ. 5), Jianliao (SJ. 14), Yifeng (SJ. 17), Ermen (SJ. 21) and Erheliao (SJ. 22). Acupuncturists and Qigong masters should recite all the points.

Locations of the important points: (Fig. SJ.-2)

1. Guanchong: On the side of the ring finger, about 0.1 cun behind the corner of the nail.
2. Yemen: Proximal to the margin of the web between the ring and small fingers.
4. Yangchi: At the junction of the ulna and carpal bones, in the depression beside the extensor digitorum communis tendon.
5. Waiguan: Two cun above Yangchi, between the radius and ulna.
10. Tianjing: When the elbow is flexed, the point is in the depression about 1 cun above the olecranon.
14. Jianliao: Behind and below the acromion, in the depression about 1 cun behind to Jianyu.
17. Yifeng: Behind the lobule of the ear, in the depression between the mandible and mastoid process.
21. Ermen: In the depression in front of the supratragic notch and slightly superior to the condyloid process of the mandible. The point is located with the mouth open.
22. Erheliao: In front of and above Ermen, level with the root of the auricle, on the posterior border of the hairline of the temple, where the superficial

temporal artery passes.

23. Sizhukong: In the depression at the lateral end of the eyebrow.

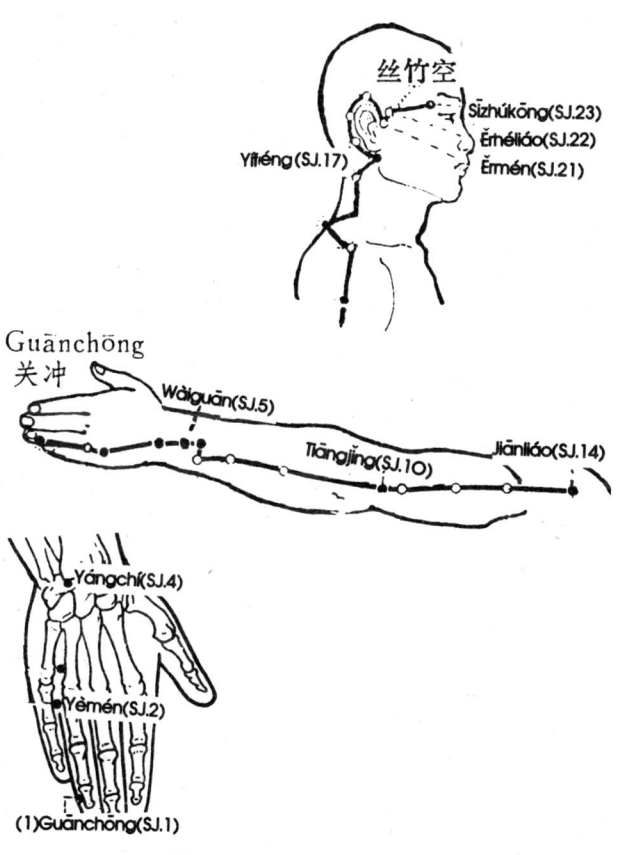

Fig.SJ.-2 The Sānjiāo Meridian of Hand-Shàoyáng

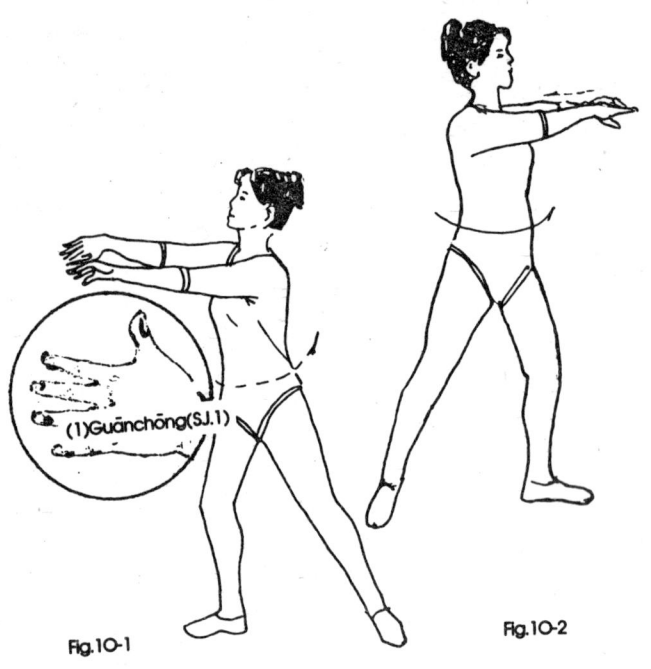

Fig. 10-1   Fig. 10-2

Instructions:

1. Turn the body and stretch the arms out to the right (Fig. 10-1).

Turn the trunk and the right foot 90 to the right. At the same time stretch out the arms to the right. Put the right index finger on the left ring finger. The weight is on the right foot. Take a step backward with the left foot. Breathe normally.

2. Turn the left to move the Qi of the left side (Figs. 10-2, 10-3).

Gradually turn the trunk, the right foot 135 degrees

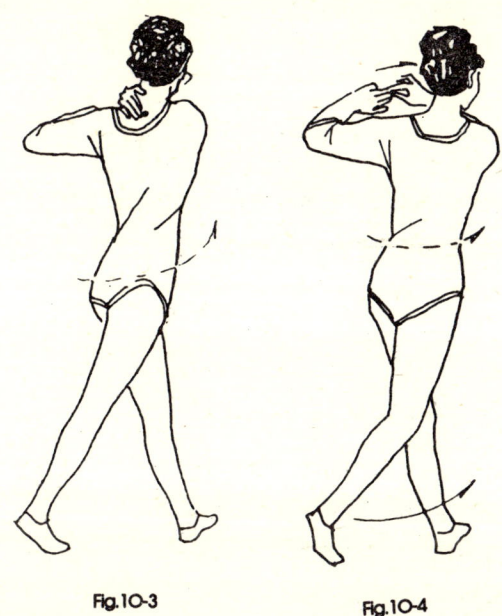

Fig.10-3   Fig.10-4

and the left foot 90 degrees to the left while moving the Qi along the meridian. When the Qi has been moved to Dazhui, bend the left arm. Turn the left foot 45 and the trunk to the left. Take a step forward with the right foot. Put the left index finger on the right ring finger.

Notes:

While exhaling move the Qi from the starting point to the elbow.

While inhaling move the Qi from the elbow to the Dazhui point.

3. Turn to the right to move the Qi of the right side (Figs. 10-4, 10-5, 10-6).

Fig. 10-6

Fig. 10-5

While stretching the arms out forward, turn the trunk and the right foot 45 degrees to the right. At the same time the left index finger should move the Qi upward along the right route. When the Qi has been moved to Dazhui, bend the right arm. Turn the right foot 45 degrees and the trunk to the right. Take a step forward with the left foot. Start moving the Qi of the right side.

Notes:
See the notes in action (2).
Move the Qi twice for each side.

Fig. 10-7 Fig. 10-8

4. Turn the body and raise the arms (Figs. 10-6, 10-7, 10-8, 10-9)

While exhaling turn the right foot 90 degrees and the body to the right. Move the left foot so as to keep the feet at shoulders' width. While inhaling raise the arms over the head and bring the fingers together. While exhaling, drop the hands to touch Dazhui.

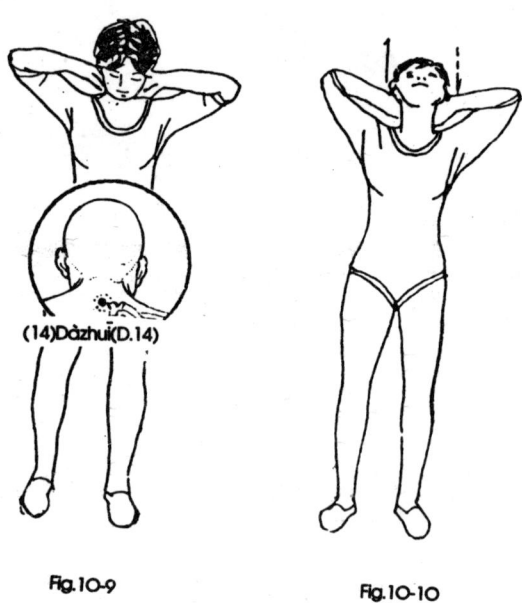

Fig. 10-9 Fig. 10-10

5. Move to Dazhui, breathe normally (Figs. 10-9, 10-10, 10-11, 10-12, 10-13, 10-14).

Nod and raise the head six times.

Fig.10-11 Fig.10-12

Turn the trunk and the limbs to the left and right six times.

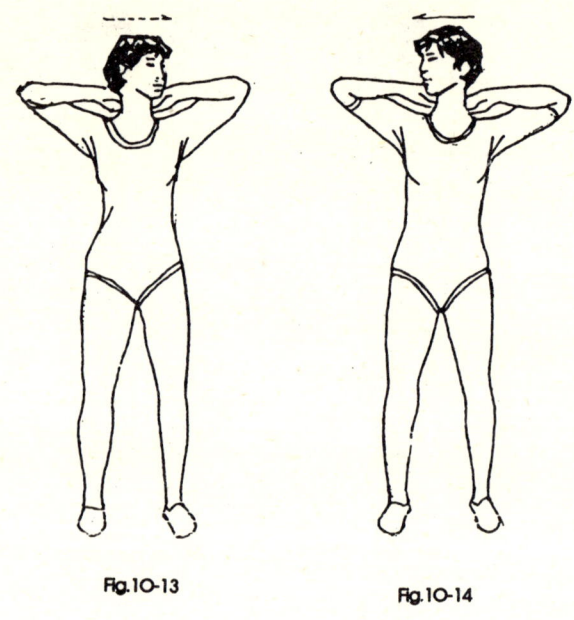

Fig.10-13   Fig.10-14

Turn the head to each side six times.

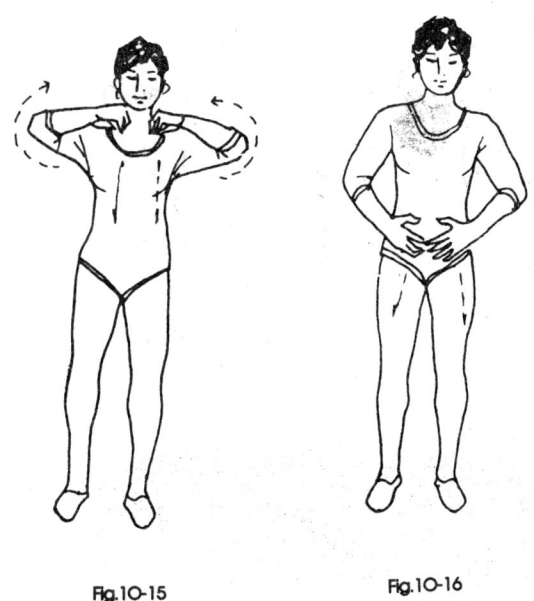

Fig. 10-15　　　　Fig. 10-16

6. Go to the supraclavicular fossa, rotate the arms three times (Fig. 10-15).

Move the hands to the supraclavicular fossa, rotate the arms from front to back three times. Breathe normally. Be aware of how the meridian branches.

7. Concentrate on Sanjiao (Fig. 10-16).

While exhaling drop the hands along the route to the lower jiao. Inhale and hold the breath.

Notes:

When moving the Qi downward, visualize the Qi in the internal branch connecting with the pericardium

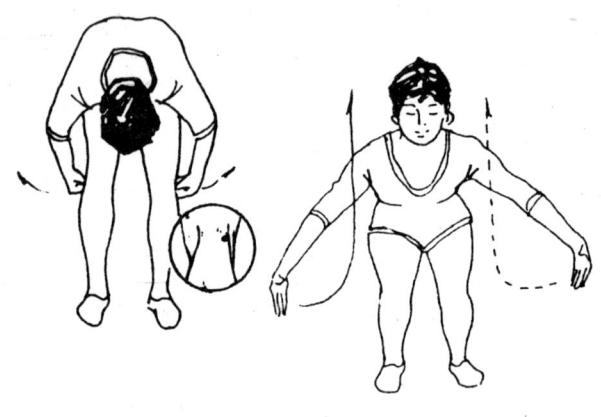

Fig. 10-17   Fig. 10-18

and descending through the diaphragm to the abdomen, where it joins its pertaining parts—the upper, middle, and lower jiao.

8 Bend over to meet the point Weiyang (Fig. 10-17).

While exhaling slowly, bend over and move the hands along the routes to Weiyang (B. 39). During this action the Qi moves from Sanjiao to Weiyang.

9. Bend the knees and hold the Qi (Fig. 10-18).

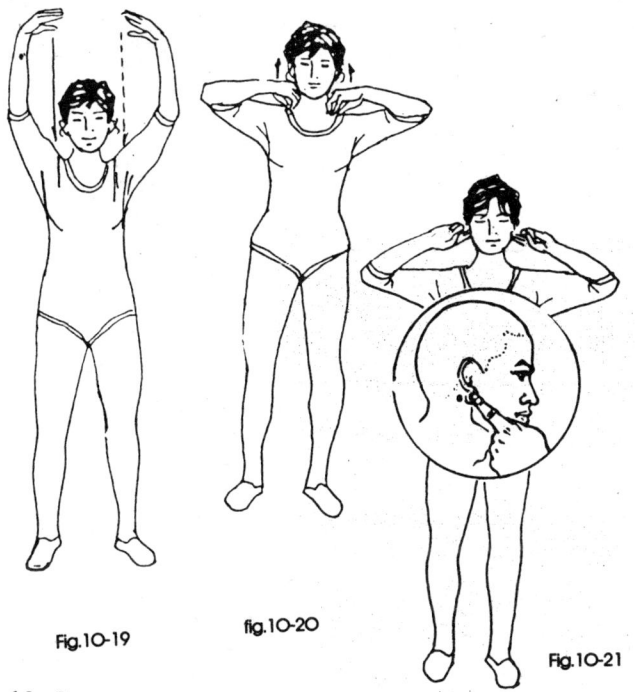

Fig. 10-19 fig. 10-20 Fig. 10-21

10. Straighten the body and lift the arms over the head (Fig. 10-19).

11. Pour the Qi into the supraclavicular fossa (Fig. 10-20).

12. Massage Yifeng six times (Fig. 10-21).

While inhaling move the hands upward along the superficial branch to Yifeng (SJ.17). Place the middle fingers on the index fingers. Massage Yifeng with the fingers six times. In the mind, visualize the Qi entering the ears and connecting with the eyes. Breathe normally.

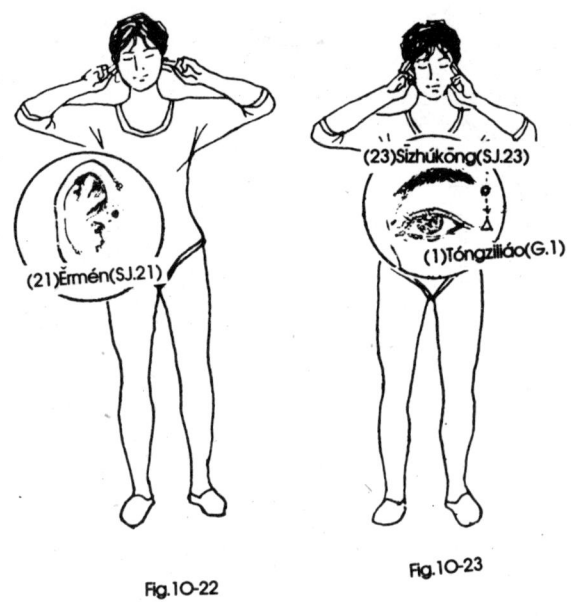

Fig.10-22   Fig.10-23

13. Massage Ermen and Erheliao six times (Fig. 10-22).

The fingers go upward to Ermen and Erheliao. Put the index fingers and the middle fingers on Ermen and Erheliao respectively, and massage them six times. Breathe normally.

14. Massage Sizhukong (Fig. 10-23).

Move the fingers to Sizhukong. Massage Sizhukong six times. The mind should move the Qi downward to the outer canthi Tongziliao to link with the Gall Bladder Meridian of the Foot-Shaoyang.

XI. The Gall Bladder Meridian of the Foot-Shaoyang

Flow route: (Fig. G.-1)

The Gall Bladder Meridian of the Foot-Shaoyang starts from the outer canthus (Tongziliao, G.1), goes obliquely to Tinghui, ascends to the corner of the forehead (Touwei, S. 8), then descends around the back of the ear to Wangu (G. 12). From there, returning to the forehead, it reaches Yangbai (G. 14). It then descends to Fengchi (G. 20). There two branches emerge. The internal one enters the ear by passing Yifeng (SJ. 17). Then it comes out and meets Tongziliao. Descending to the cheek and back to a point below the eye, it goes downward along the neck to the supraclavicular fossa, where it meets the superficial branch. From there the internal branch further descends into the chest, passes through the diaphragm to connect with the liver, and enters its pertaining organ, the gall bladder. From there it runs downward to the edge of the pubic hair, where it goes transversely into the hip region (Huantiao, G. 30). The superficial branch goes downward from Fengchi to Tianrong (SI. 17). Then it goes back to meet the Dazhui point. From Dazhui, passing Jianjing, it reaches the supraclavicular fossa. It runs downward from the supraclavicular fossa, passes the front of the axilla along the lateral aspect of the chest and through the free ends of the floating ribs to the hip region, where it finally joins the internal branch. Descending along the mid-line of the lateral aspect of the leg, passing Zulinqi (G. 41), it reaches the side of the tip of the fourth toe.

A branch from Zulinqi runs to the hairy region of the big toe, where it links with the Liver Meridian of

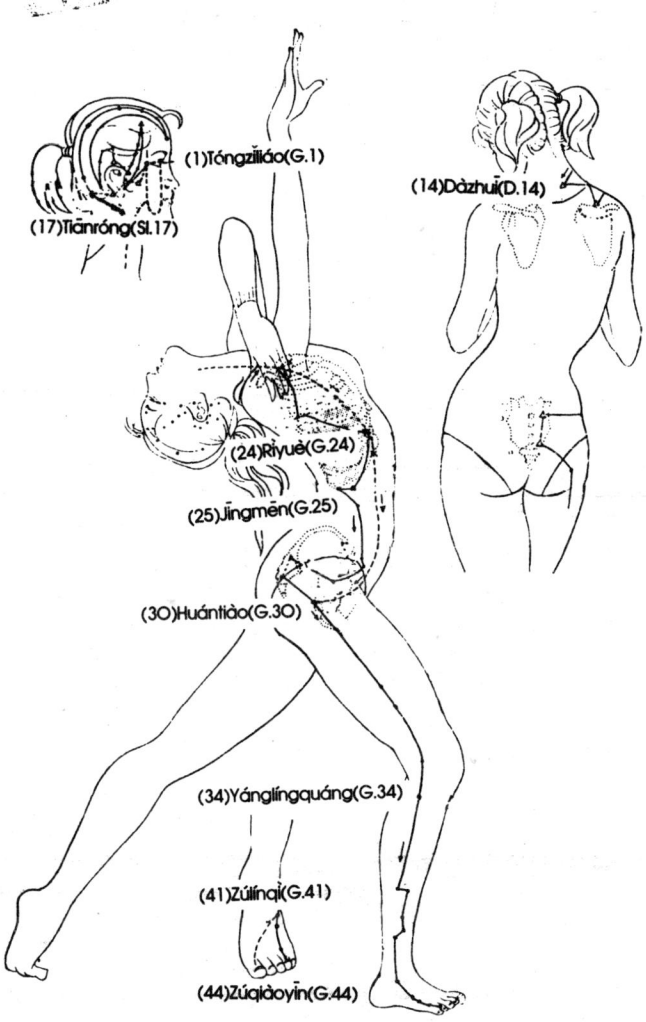

Fig.G.-1　The Gall Bladder Meridian of Foot-Shàoyáng

the Foot-Jueyin.

Indications:

Sensation of fullness of the chest and hypochondria region, bitter taste in mouth, ache on one side of the head, frequent sighing and moodiness, pain in the side of the leg, numb feet, spontaneous sweating and chronic cholecystitis.

Requirements:

Be clearly aware of the important points and the route on the head. The Gall Bladder Meridian goes from the head to the foot. While moving the Qi along the meridian, concentrate on regulating the mind, the respiration and the strength of the actions. breathe in and out slowly and deeply.

Three keypoints:

1. The three turnings on the head should be known.
2. The two branches emerge at Fengchi and join together at Huantiao.
3. A branch emerges at Zulinqi, and it meets the Liver Meridian. There are altogether 44 points. Remember the starting point Tongziliao and the ending point Zuqiaoyin, in additio to Tinghui (G. 2), Wangu (G. 12), Yangbai (G. 14), Fengchi (G. 20) and Zulinqi (G. 41). Acupuncturists and Qigong masters should recite all the points silently while moving the Qi.

Location of the important points: (Fig. G.-2)

1. Tóngziliáo: Beside the outer canthus, in the depression on the lateral side of the orbit.

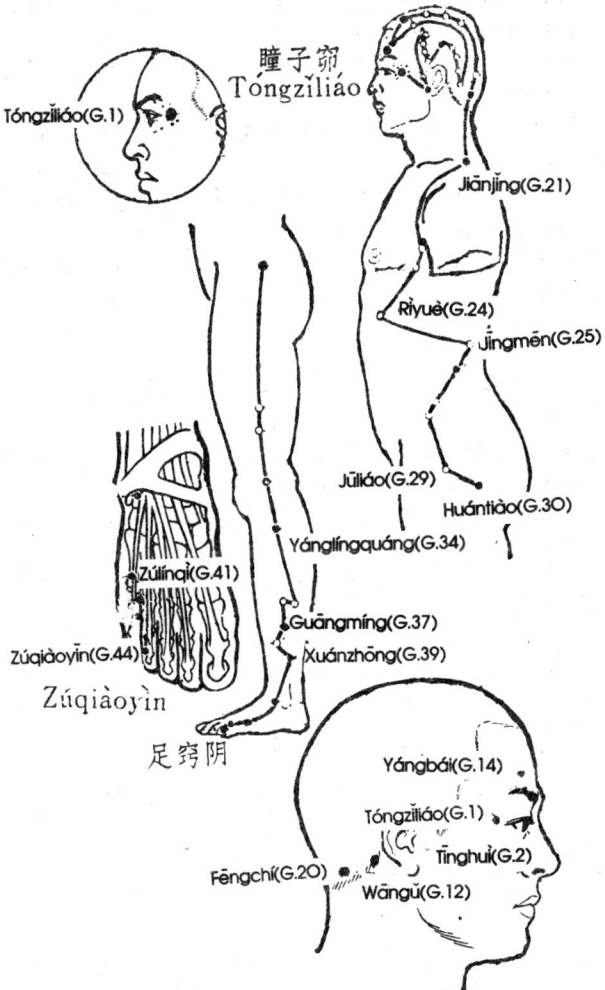

Fig.G.-2 The Gall Bladder Meridian of Foot-Shàoyáng

2. Tinghui: In front of the intertragic notch, directly below Tinggong, at the posterior border of the condyloid process of the mandible. The point is located with the mouth open.

12. Wangu: In the depression behind and below the mastoid process.

14. Yangbai: On the forehead, 1 cun above the midpoint of the eyebrow.

20. Fengchi: In the posterior aspect of the neck, below the occipital bone, in the depression between the upper portion of sternocleidomastoideus muscle and the trapezius.

21. Jianjing: Midway between Dazhui and the acromion, at the highest point of the shoulder.

24. Riyue: Inferior to the nipple, between the cartilage of the seventh and eighth ribs.

25. Jingmen: On the side of the abdomen, on the lower border of the free end of the twelfth rib.

29. Juliao: Midway between the anterosuperior iliac spine and the great trochanter.

30. Huantiao: At the junction of the middle and lateral third of the distance between the great trochanter and the hiatus of the sacrum.

34. Yanglingquan: In the depression in front of and below the head of the fibula.

37. Guangming: Five cun directly above the tip of the external malleolus, on the anterior border of the fibula.

39. Xuanzhong: Three cun above the tip of the external malleolus, on the posterior border of the fibula.

41. Zulinqi: In the depression distal to the junction of the fourth and fifth metatarsal bones, on the side of

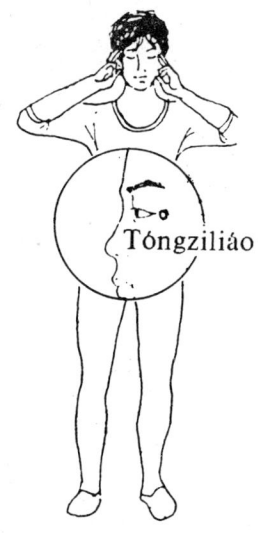

Fig.11-1

the foots of extensor digiti minimi tendon.

44. Zuqiaoyin: On the side of the fourth toe, about 0.1 cun behind the corner of the nail.

Instructions:

1 Massage Tongziliao (Fig. 11-1).
Place the middle fingers on the index fingers. Massage Tongziliao with the fingers six times. Breathe normally.

Fig.11-2

2. Massage Tinghui, Touwei and Wangu (Figs. 11-2, 11-3, 11-4).

Moving along the route, the fingers massage Tinghui, Touwei and Wangu six times at each point. Breathe naturally.

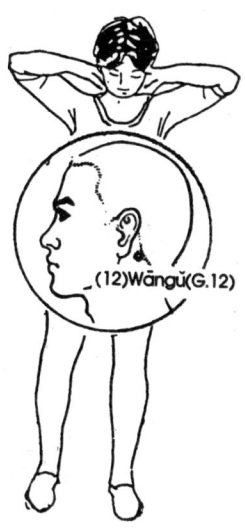

Fig.11-4

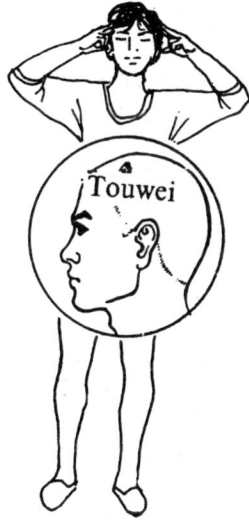

Fig.11-3

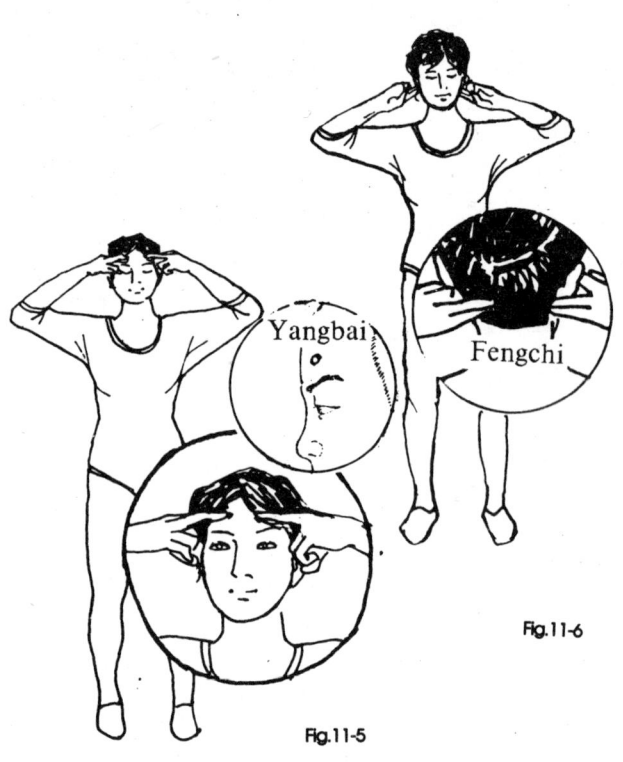

Fig.11-5

Fig.11-6

3. Massage Yangbai (Fig. 11-5).

The fingers go upward along the route to Yangbai. Massage Yangbai six times. Breathe naturally.

4. Massage Fengchi (Fig. 11-6).

Move along the route, the fingers reach Fengchi and massage it six times. Breathe normally.

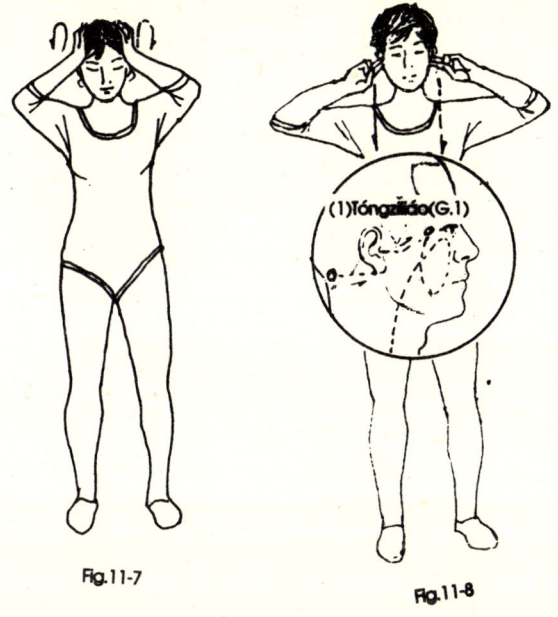

Fig.11-7

Fig.11-8

5. Massage the head (Fig. 11-7).

The palms massage the temporal bones from the front to the back six times. Breathe normally.

6. Descend to enter the gall bladder and connect with the liver (Figs. 11-8, 11-9).

The fingers move along the internal branch. The fingers reach Yifeng and go through the ears and back to Tongziliao again. Go around the cheeks to points below the eyes. While exhaling move the Qi downward

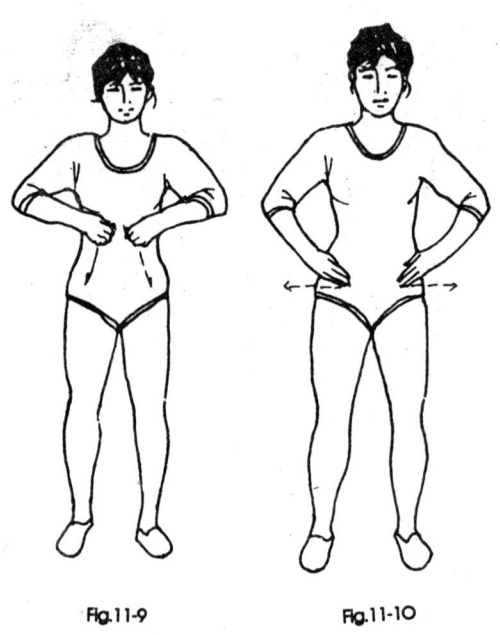

Fig.11-9   Fig.11-10

to enter the gall bladder and connect with the liver.
Note:
The mind should follow the Qi along its internal route.

7. Go downward to the groin (Fig. 11-10).

While exhaling, drop the hands along the routes to the groins.

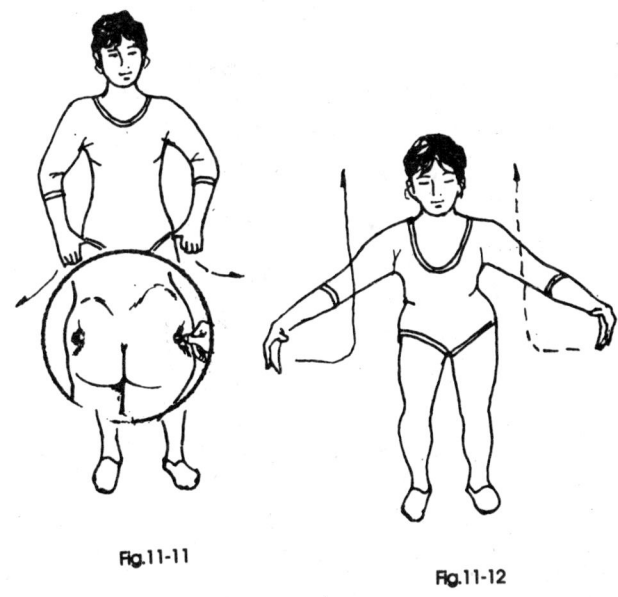

Fig.11-11

Fig.11-12

8. Go transversely into the hip region (Fig. 11-11).
While inhaling move the hands from the edge of the pubic hair transversely to the hip region Huantiao point (G. 30).

9. Bend the knees and hold the Qi (Fig. 11-12).

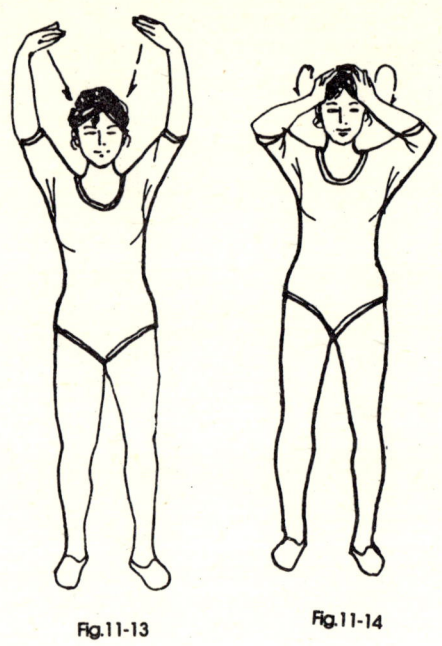

Fig.11-13   Fig.11-14

10. Straighten the body and lift the arms over the head (Fig. 11-13). Massage the head three times. (Fig. 11-14).

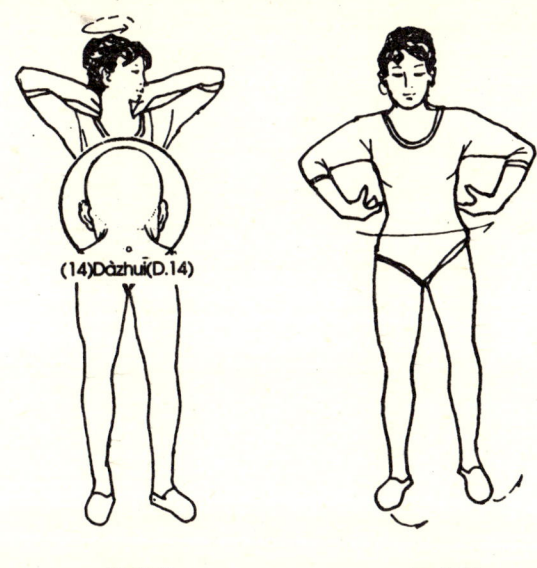

Fig.11-15　　　　　Fig.11-16

11. Meet with Dazhui (Fig. 11-15).

The hands move from Fengchi to Tianrong (SI. 17) and then go to meet with Dazhui. Breathe normally.

12. Move Dazhui (Fig. 11-15).

Rotate Dazhui clockwise six times and counterclockwise six times. Breathe normally.

13. Move the Qi to the axillae (Fig. 11-16).

Move the hands past the Jianjing point (G. 21) to the supraclavicular fossa and then move the Qi into the axillae. Stretch the arms out to the back. Turn the right foot 45 degrees and the left foot 90 degrees to the left. The body follows the feet and faces the left side. Inhale slowly during the movements.

Fig.11-17

Fig.11-18

14. Move the Qi along the left meridian (Fig. 11-17)

Bend the arms. While bending over, the hands move the Qi along the route to the ending point Zuqiaoyin. Exhale slowly during this movement.

15. Straighten the body, lift the arms and massage the head (Fig. 11-18).

While inhaling slowly straighten the body and lift the arms over the head. While exhaling drop the arms to massage the temporal bones three times. While inhaling move the Qi into the axillas and then stretch the arms out to the back.

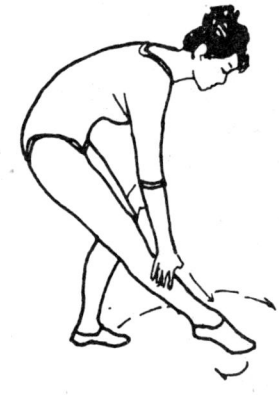

Fig.11-19

16. Move the Qi along the right meridian (Fig. 11-19).

Take a step forward with the right foot. While bending over, the hands move the Qi along the route to the ending point Zuqiaoyin. Exhale slowly during this movement.

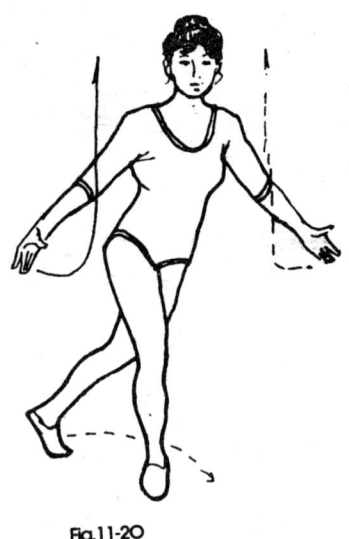

Fig.11-20

17. Straighten, lift the arms and turn the body (Figs. 11-20, 11-21, 11-22).

While inhaling, slowly straighten the body and lift the arms over the head. Turn the right foot 90 degrees

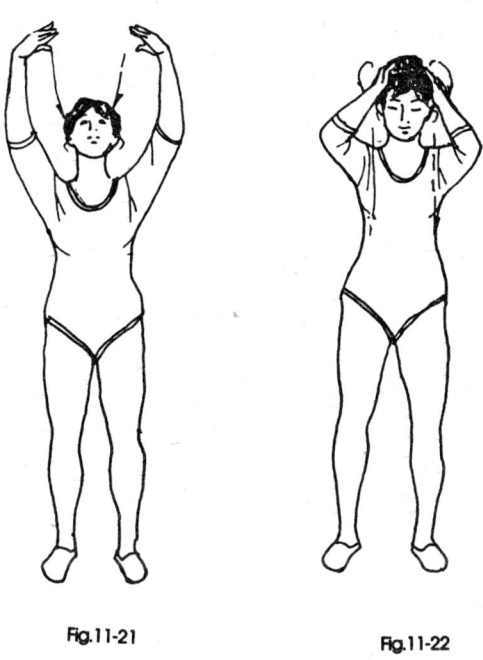

Fig.11-21 Fig.11-22

and the body to the right. Move the left foot so as to keep the feet at shoulders' width. While exhaling drop the arms to massage the temporal bones three times.

18. Move the Qi to the axillas (Fig. 11-23)

Move the hands to the axillae, then stretch the arms out to the back. Turn the left foot 45 degrees and the right foot 90 degrees to the right. The body follows the feet and faces the right side. Inhale slowly during the movement.

19. Move the Qi along the right meridian and left meridian (Figs. 11-24, 11-25, 11-26).

See actions (14), (15), (16).

20. Straighten, lift the arms and turn the body (Figs. 11-27, 11-28).

While inhaling, slowly straighten up and lift the

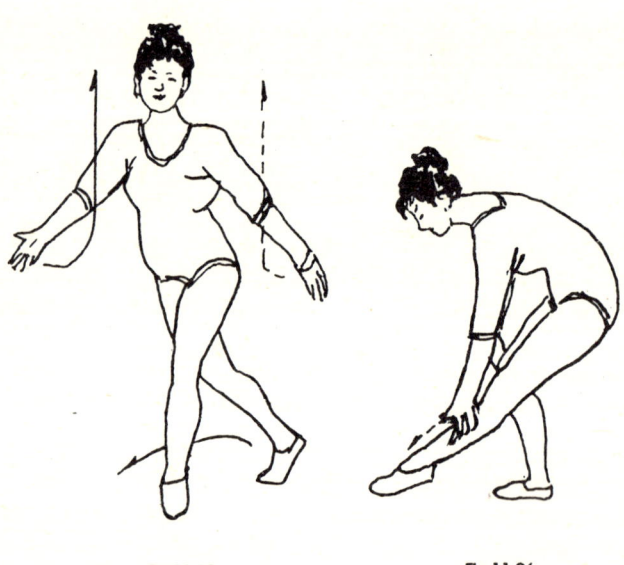

Fig.11-27   Fig.11-26

Fig.11-24   Fig.11-23

Fig.11-25

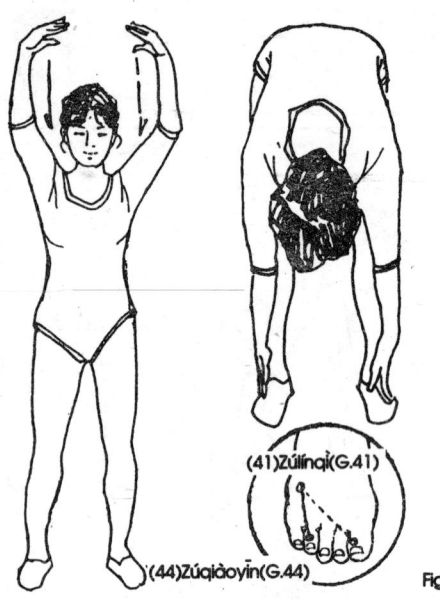

Fig.11-28 Fig.11-29

arms over the head. Turn the left foot 90 degrees and rotate the body to the left. Move the right foot so as to keep the feet at shoulders' width. While exhaling, drop the arms. Massage the temporal bone three times, with natural breathing.

21. Move the bilateral Qi and link with the liver meridian (Fig. 11-29).

While inhaling, with the hands move the Qi to the axillae. While exhaling, bend over slowly moving the Qi downward along the routes. When the Qi reaches Zulinqi, it will then move along the branch to the big toes' Dadun (Liv. 1), where it links with the Liver Meridian of the Foot-Jueyin.

XII. The Liver Meridian of the Foot-Jueyin

Flow route: (Fig. Liv.-1)

The Liver Meridian of the Foot-Jueyin starts from the side of the tip of the big toe (Dadun, Liv. 1). Running upward along the dorsum of the foot, passing through Zhongfeng (Liv. 4) 1 cun from the center of the ankle, it ascends to the medial side of the knee. It further runs upward along the medial aspect of the thigh to the pubic hair region, where it curves around the external genitals and then goes up to the lower abdomen until it reaches Qimen (Liv. 14) by passing Zhangmen (Liv. 13). From Zhangmen it branches into the abdomen. Then it runs upward, curves around the stomach to enter the liver, its pertaining organ, and connects with the gall bladder. From there it continues to ascend, passing through the diaphragm and branching out into the costal and hypochondrial regions. Then it ascends along the throat to the nasopharynx and opens into the eyes. Running further upward, it enters the brain, goes through the ears and emerges from the forehead to meet the Du Meridian at the vertex.

The branch which arises from the "eye system" runs downward into the cheek and curves around the inner surface of the lips. The Qi spreads on the sides of the tongue.

The other branch arising from the liver passes through the diaphragm, flows into the lungs and goes downward to the middle jiao, where it links with the Lung Meridian of the Hand-Taiyin.

Indications:

Headache, dizziness, blurring of vision, sore throat,

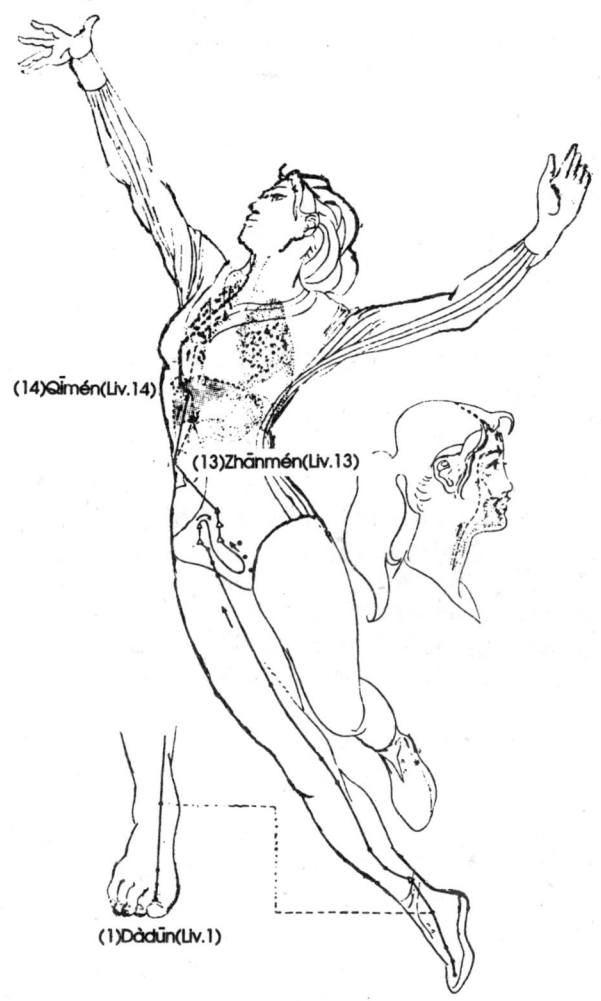

Fig.Liv.-1　The Liver Meridian of Foot Juéyīn

distention and fullness in the chest and hypochondrial region. Pain in the lower abdomen, fatigue and hypertension.

Requirements:

Concentrate on regulating the respiration and balancing. The meridian goes from the foot to the chest. There are altogether 14 points. Remember the starting point Dadun and the ending point Qimen, as well as Taichong (Liv. 3) and Zhangmen (Liv. 13).

Acupuncturists and Qigong masters should remember all the points.

Locations of the important points: (Fig. Liv-2)

1. Dadun: On the side of the dorsum of the terminal phalanx of the big toe, between the lateral corner of the nail and interphalangeal joint.

2. Xingjian: Between the first and second toes, near the margin of the web.

3. Taichong: In the depression distal to the junction of the first and second metatarsal bones.

7. Xiguan: Behind and below the medial condylus of the tibia, on the upper portion of the medial head of the gastrocnemius muscle, 1 cun behind Yinlinquan (Sp. 9).

8. Ququan: On the medial side of the knee joint. When the knee is flexed, the point is above the medial end of the transverse popliteal crease, behind the medial condylus of the tibia, on the front border of the insertion of m. semimembranosus and m. semitendinosus.

12. Jimai: Below and to the side of the pubic spine,

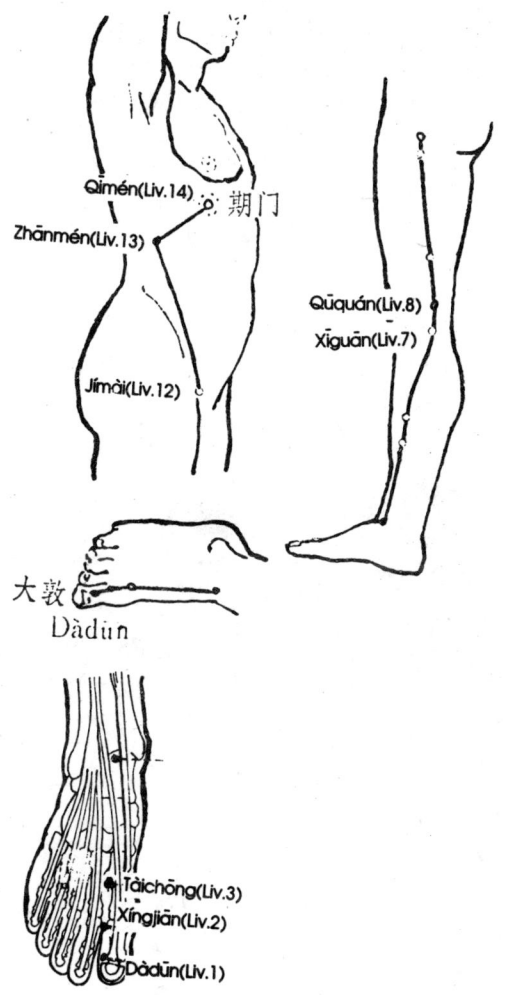

Fig.Liv.-2　The Liver Meridian of Foot-Juéyīn

2.5 cun from the Ren Meridian, at the inguinal groove beside and below Qichong (S. 30).

13. Zhangmen: To the side of the abdomen, below the free end of the eleventh floating rib.

14. Qimen: On the mammillary line, two ribs below the nipple, in the sixth intercostal space.

Instructions:

Fig.12-4   Fig.12-3

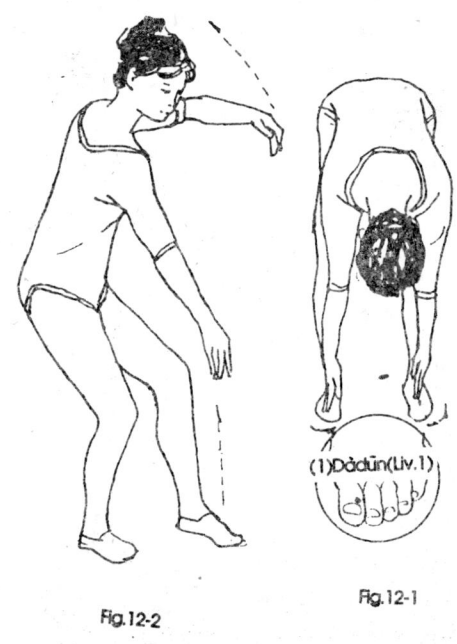

Fig. 12-1

Fig. 12-2

1. Turn the body to the left and move the Qi along the left route (Figs. 12-1, 12-2, 12-3).

Slowly straighten the body from the bending position. Turn the right foot 45 and the left foot 90 degrees to the left. The body faces left. Raise the left arm and leg. At the same time stretch the right arm to the left foot. Concentrate on the starting point. While inhaling, move the Qi upward along the route.

2. Move the Qi of the left route and take a step backward with the left foot (Figs. 12-4, 12-5).

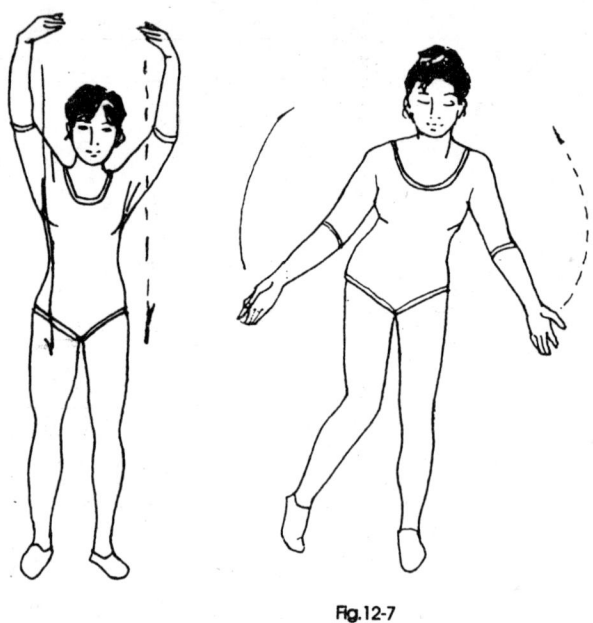

Fig. 12-7

Fig. 12-8

When the Qi has been moved to the pubic region, step backward with the left foot. Continue to move the Qi upward along the route to Qimen (Liv. 14). At this point the inhalation is finished.

Note:

Remember to move the Qi externally around the genitals.

3. Raise the right arm and leg (Figs. 12-5, 12-6).

While exhaling raise the right arm and leg and drop the left arm. Stretch the left arm to the right foot. Concentrate on the starting point.

Fig. 12-6   Fig. 12-5

4. Move the Qi of the right route and take a step backward with the right foot (Fig. 12-6).

While inhaling, move the Qi upward to the pubic region. Take a step backward with the right foot. Move the Qi around the external genitals to Qimen (Liv. 14). While exhaling drop the right arm and raise the left arm and leg to move the Qi of the left side again.

Move the Qi twice along the route of each side.

5. Turn the body and raise the arms (Figs. 12-7, 12-8).

While continuing to exhale, turn the body to the

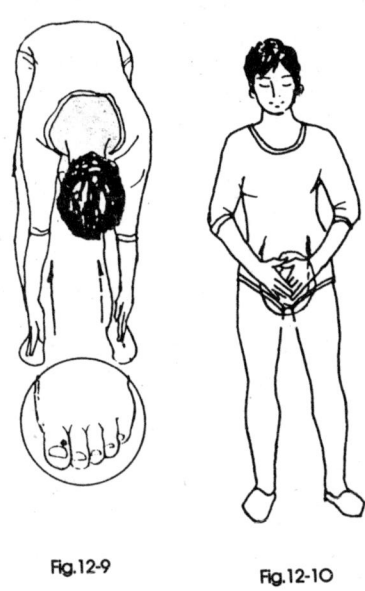

Fig. 12-9 Fig. 12-10

right. While inhaling, gradually raise the arms from the back. Move the right foot so as to keep the feet at shoulders' width.

6. Move the bilateral Qi (Fig. 12-9).

While exhaling bend over and with hands touch the starting points. While inhaling, with the hands slowly move the Qi upward along the routes, as the body slowly straightens.

7. Go around the genitals (Fig. 12-10).

While you exhale, the hands move the Qi around the genitals.

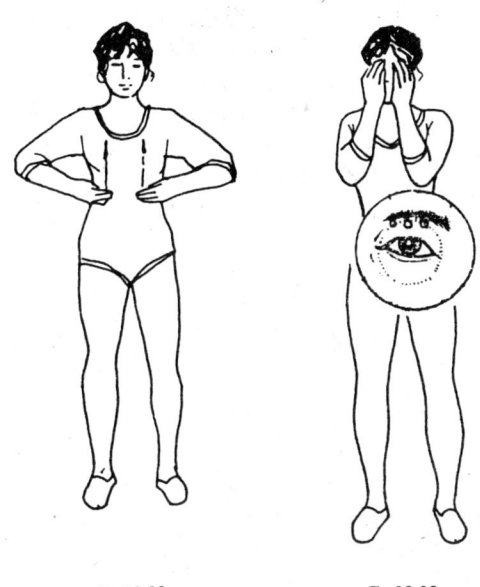

Fig.12-11 Fig.12-12

8. Enter the liver and connect with the gall bladder (Fig. 12-11).

While you inhale, the Qi is moved to Qimen (Liv. 14). It enters the liver and connects with the gall bladder. Move the hands upward along the routes to the eyes. In the mind, visualize the Qi along the routes to the eyes. In the mind, visualize the Qi opening into the eyes and entering the brain.

9. Massage the eyeballs (Fig. 12-12).

Place the middle fingers on the eyeballs, and the index fingers and ring fingers on the sides of the eyeballs. Massage the eyeballs six times. Concentrate on the Qi going to the brain. Breathe normally.

Fig. 12-13

10. Go around the mouth and spread over the tongue (Fig. 12-13).

Move the hands downward to the mouth. Visualize the Qi going through the cheeks and around the lips. Massage the mouth back and forth with the index fingers six times. Visualize the Qi spreading along the sides of the tongue. Breathe normally.

Fig 12-14

11. Go to the vertex, enter the brain and go through the ears (Fig. 12-14).

Move the hands from the mouth upward to the vertex. Use the middle fingers to press Baihui (D. 20) six times. Visualize the Qi entering the brain and going through the ears. Breathe normally.

Fig.12-15

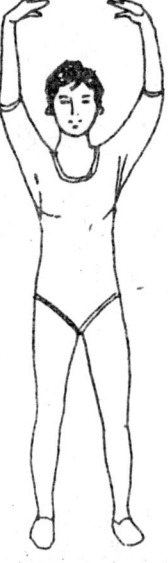

Fig.12-16

12. Bend the knees and hold the Qi.
13. Straighten the body and lift the arms over the head.

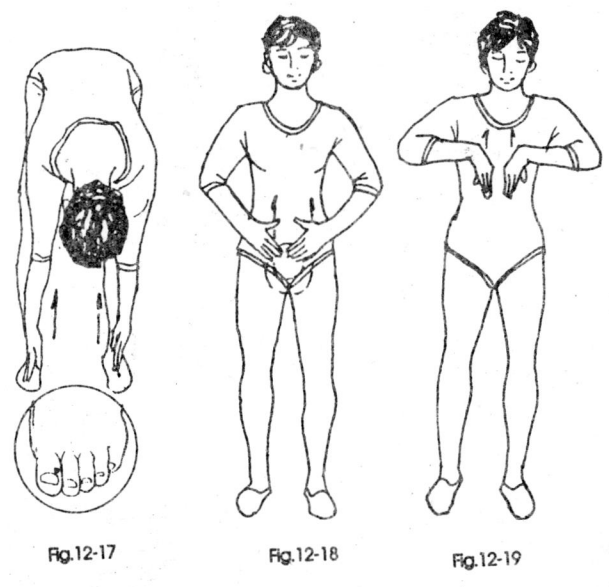

Fig.12-17   Fig.12-18   Fig.12-19

14. Move the bilateral Qi (Fig. 12-17).

15. Go around the genitals and upward (Figs. 12-18, 12-19).

As you inhale, the hands move the Qi around the genitals.

As you exhale, the Qi is moved upward to enter the upper abdomen.

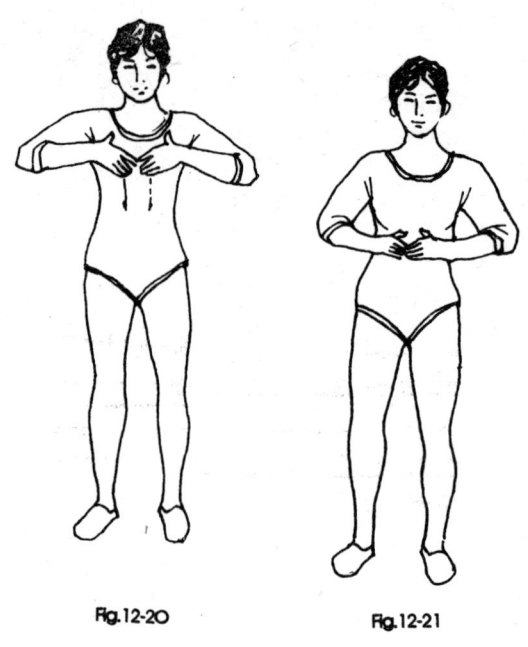

Fig. 12-20   Fig. 12-21

16. Flow into the lungs (Figs. 12-20, 12-21).

With the hands move the Qi to the lungs. Passing downward through the diaphragm, move the hands back to the middle jiao to the starting position of the Lung Meridian.

Notes:
While inhaling, move the Qi upward.
While exhaling, move the Qi downward.
17. Concentrate on Dantian.

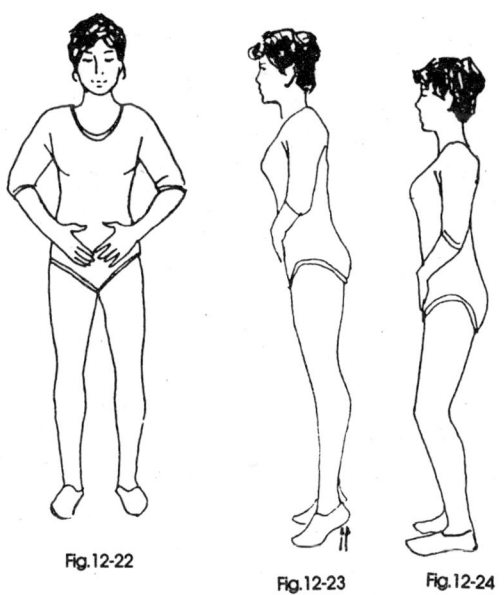

Fig.12-22

Fig.12-23　　Fig.12-24

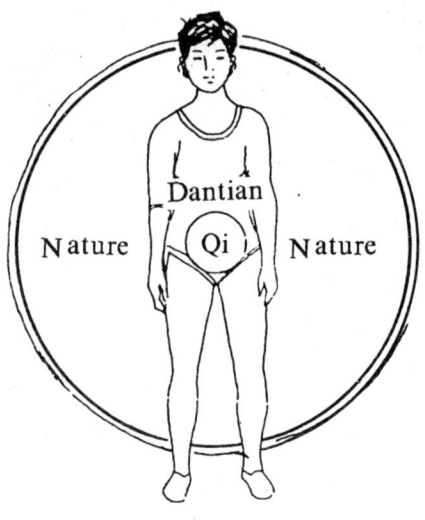

Fig.12-25

(小周天)

任 ⇌ 督

Ren Meridian (R)   Du Meridian (D)

XIII. The Ren Meridian

The Ren Meridian controls all the Yin Meridians of the body; therefore it is called the "Sea of Yin" Meridian. It is also related to the reproductive and sexual functions.

Flow route: (Fig. R.-1)

The Ren Meridian arises from Dantian and emerges from the perineum (Huiyin, R. 1). It runs back to curve around the external genitals and reaches the mons pubis. Ascending along the mid-line of the abdomen, thorax and nucha (nape of the neck), it reaches the Chengjiang point (R. 24) below the lower lip. Then it curves around the lips and reaches Yinjiao (D. 28). Merging with the Du Meridian, it branches and ascends along the cheeks to the Chengqi points (S. 1) below the eyes, where the Qi enters the brain.

Indications:

Move the Qi to the hypogastrium (lower abdomen) and massage that part to relieve problems of the genito-urinary system, such as hernia, leucorrhea, abdominal mass, irregular menstruation, seminal emission, premature ejaculation, and impotence.

Move the Qi to the epigastrium (upper abdomen) and massage that part for treating enteropathy (intestinal disorders) and gastropathy (stomach disorders).

Move the Qi to the thorax and massage that part for treating problems of the heart, lungs and upper esophagus.

Requirements:

Fig.R.-1 The Ren Meridian

Concentrate on regulating the respiration and moving the Qi along the meridian. Massage Shenque (R. 8), Zhongwan (R. 12), Tanzhong (R. 17), Chengjiang (R. 24) and Chengqi (S. 1) sequentially. There are altogether 24 points distributed on the mid-line of the thorax and abdomen. Remember the starting Huiyin point and the ending Chengjiang point, besides the five points mentioned above. Acupuncturists and Qigong masters should recite all the points silently while moving the Qi.

Location of the important points:

1. Huiyin: At the center of the perineum. It lies between the anus and the scrotum in males and between the anus and the posterior labial commissure in females.

3. Zhongji: On the anterior mid-line, 4 cun below the umbilicus and 1 cun above the upper border of the symphysis pubis.

4. Guanyuan: On the mid-line of the abdomen, 3 cun below the umbilicus.

6. Qihai: On the mid-line of the abdomen and 1.5 cun below the umbilicus.

8. Shenque: In the center of the umbilicus.

12. Zhongwan: On the mid-line of the abdomen, 4 cun above the umbilicus.

17. Tanzhong: On the mid-line of the sternum, between the nipples, level with the fourth intercostal space.

22. Tiantu: At the center of the suprasternal fossa.

24. Chengjiang: In the depression at the center of the mentolabial groove.

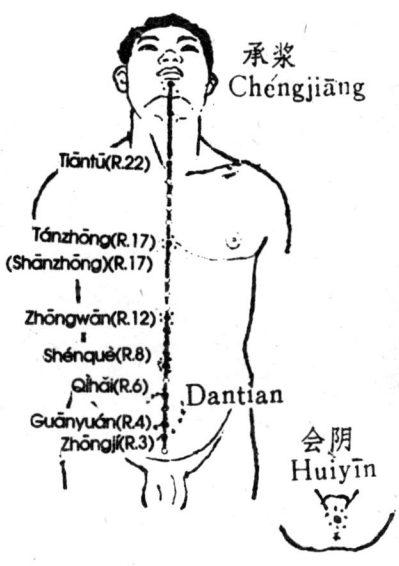

Fig.R.-2 The Ren Meridian

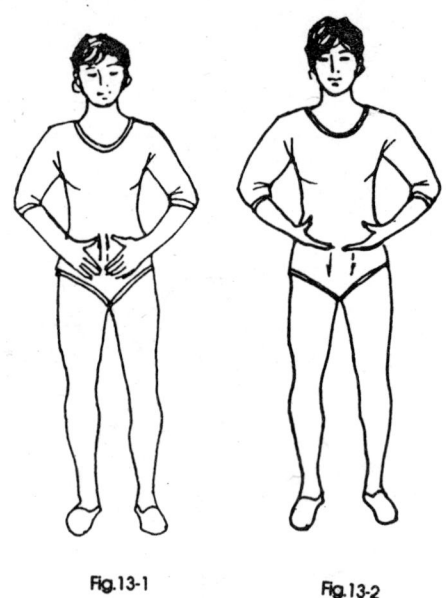

Fig. 13-1   Fig. 13-2

Instructions:

1. Start from Dantian, emerge from Huiyin (Figs. 13-1, 13-2, 13-3).

The palms touch Dantian. While inhaling, turn the palms face up and raise them slightly. Then while exhaling, turn the palms face down and drop them slightly. At the same time, bend the knees slightly. In the mind visualize the Qi reaching Huiyin.

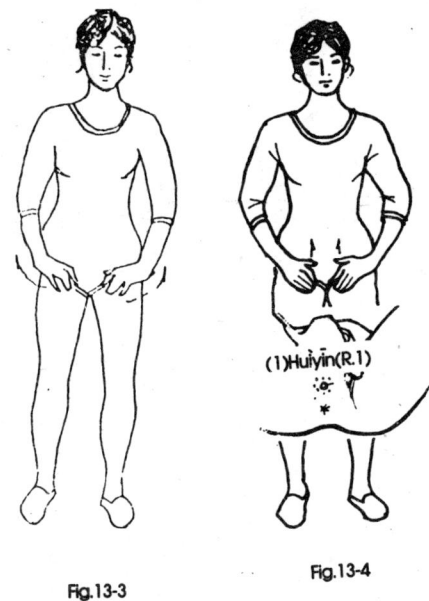

Fig.13-3　　　　Fig.13-4

2. Move the Qi around the external genitals and to Shenque (Figs. 13-3, 13-4, 13-5).

In the mind the Qi curves around the external genitals. While inhaling, straighten the knees and move the hands upward along the route to Shenque. While breathing normally, press Shenque, tense the muscles of the abdomen, contract the muscles around the genitals and anus, and clench the teeth. Do this three times.

Fig.13-5   Fig.13-6

3. Move the Qi to Zhongwan to invigorate the function of the spleen and stomach (Fig. 13-6).

While inhaling, with hands move the Qi upward to Zhongwan. While breathing normally, press Zhongwan three times.

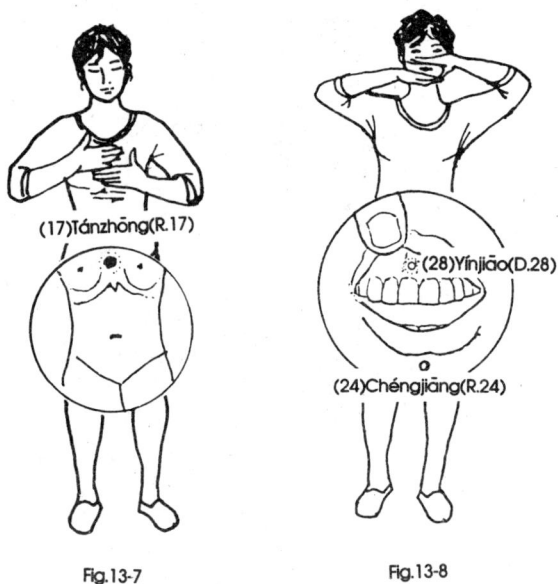

Fig.13-7   Fig.13-8

4. Move the Qi to Tanzhong to regulate the vital energy and the heart (Fig. 13-7).

While inhaling move the Qi upward to Tanzhong (between the breasts). While breathing normally, rub Tanzhong transversely three times, so as to regulate the vital energy and the heart.

5. Curve around the lips to link with the Du Meridian (Fig. 13-8).

While inhaling, move the hands upward along the route. The Qi curves around the lips and links with the Du Meridian. While breathing normally, massage the lips back and forth three times.

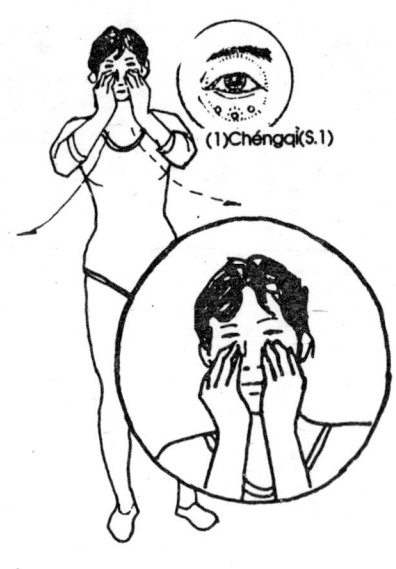

Fig. 13-9

6. Reach Chengqi and massage Chengqi (Fig. 13-9).
While inhaling, move the fingers from the corners of the mouth to Chengqi (below the eyes). The middle fingers touch Chengqi. While breathing normally, massage Chengqi three times.

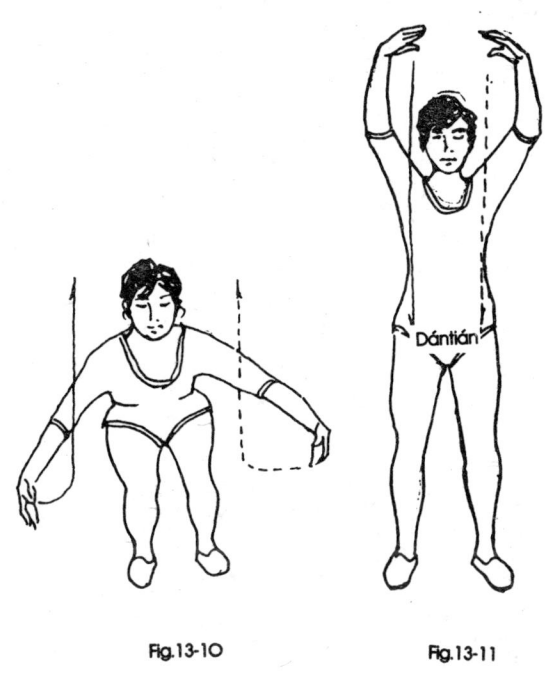

Fig. 13-10   Fig. 13-11

7. Bend the knees and hold the Qi (Fig. 13-10).
8. Straighten the body and lift the arms over the head (Fig. 13-11).

Fig. 13-12

9. Pour the Qi into Dantian (Fig. 13-12).
While exhaling, slowly drop the arms to Dantian.
While breathing normally, concentrate on Dantian.

XIV. The Du Meridian

The Du Meridian controls all the Yang Meridians of the body; therefore it is called the "Sea of Yang" Meridian.

Flow route:

The Du Meridian starts from Dantian and emerges from the perineum (Huiyin, R. 1). It runs back to curve around the anus and reaches the Changqiang point (D. 1). Ascending along the mid-line of the back, it enters the kidneys at the Mingmen point (D. 4). Passing through Dazhui (D. 14) and the nape of the neck, it reaches Fengfu (D. 16) where it enters the brain. Re-emerging, it ascends to the vertex and descends through the forehead to the tip of the nose. From the philtrum (Renzhong, D. 26), it curves around the lips and reaches Yinjiao (D. 28) where it links with the Ren Meridian.

Indications:

Sexual disorder, such as impotence, premature ejaculatio, seminal emission, irregular menstruation, hemorrhoids, functional disorder of the vegetative nerves, neurosis, insomnia, forgetfulness, dizziness, blurring of vision.

Requirements:

Concentrate on regulating the respiration and moving the Qi along the meridian. At the Mingmen point lift the kidney Qi and strenuously contract the muscles around the genitals and anus while clenching the teeth, thereby consolidating the vital energy of the kidneys. The mind should follow the Qi along the

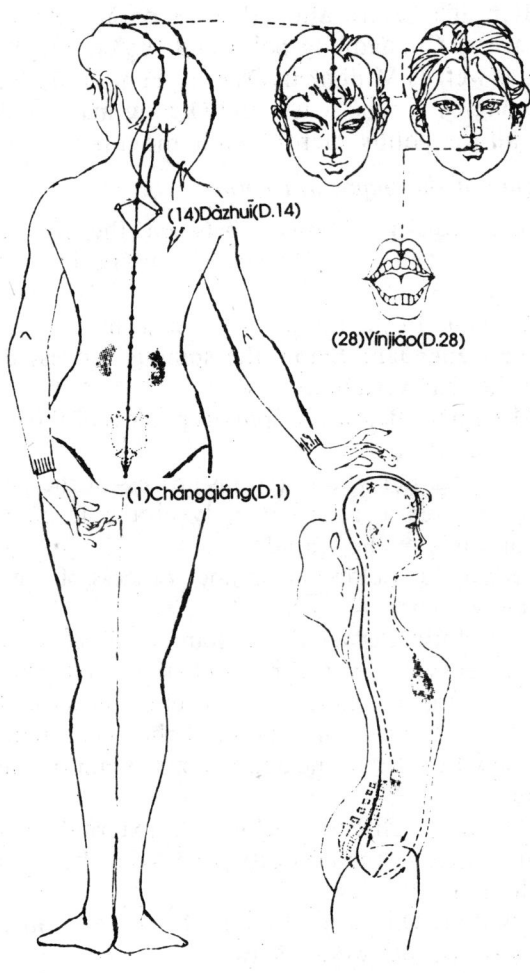

Fig.D.-1   The Du Meridian

meridian. There are altogether 28 points. Remember the starting Changqiang point and the ending Yinjiao point, as well as Mingmen, Dazhui, Fengfu, Baihui and Renzhong. Acupuncturists and Qigong masters should recite all the points silently while moving the Qi.

Location of the important points:

1. Changqiang: Midway between the tip of the coccyx and the anus. Locate the point in a prone position.

2. Yaoshu: In the hiatus of the sacrum.

3. Yaoyangguan: Below the spinous process of the fourth lumbar vertebra.

4. Mingmen: Below the spinous process of the second lumbar vertebra.

9. Zhiyang: Below the spinous process of the seventh thoracic vertebra, approximately at the level of the inferior angle of the scapula.

12. Shenzhu: Below the spinous process of the third thoracic vertebra.

14. Dazhui: Between the spinous process of the seventh cervical vertebra and the first thoracic vertebra, approximately at the level of the shoulder.

15. Yamen: At the mid-point of the neck's nape, 0.5 cun below Fengfu, in the depression 0.5 cun behind the hairline.

16. Fengfu: Directly below the external occipital protuberance, in the depression between the trapezius muscles of both sides.

20. Baihui: On the mid-point of the line connecting the apexes of the two auricles.

26. Renzhong: Below the nose, a little above the mid-point of the philtrum.

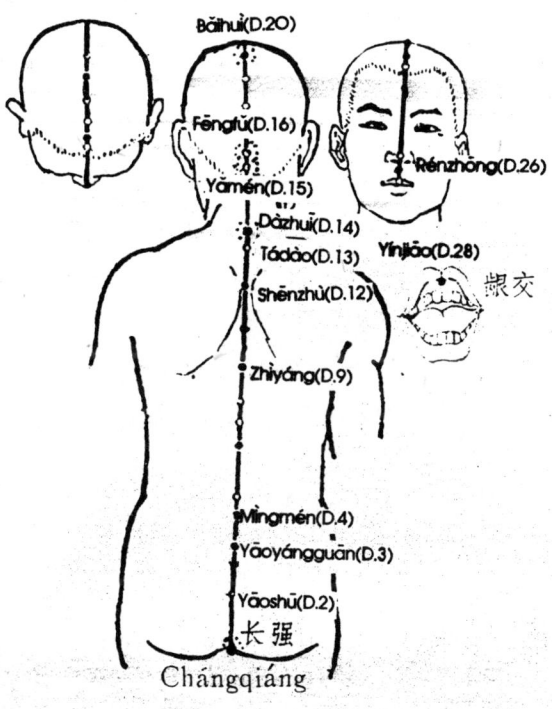

Fig.D.-2 The Du Meridian

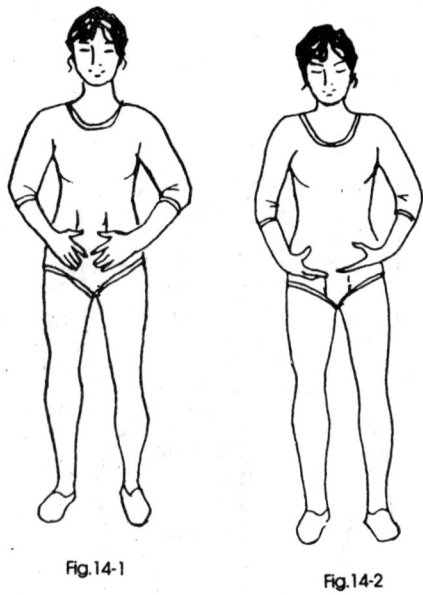

Fig.14-1   Fig.14-2

28. Yinjiao: Between the upper lip and the upper gum, in the frenum of the upper lip.

Instructions:

1. Start from Dantian, emerge from Huiyin (Figs. 14-1, 14-2).

The palms touch Dantian. While inhaling turn the palms face up and raise them slightly. Then while exhaling turn the palms face down and drop them slightly. At the same time bend the knees slightly. In the mind visualize the Qi reaching Huiyin.

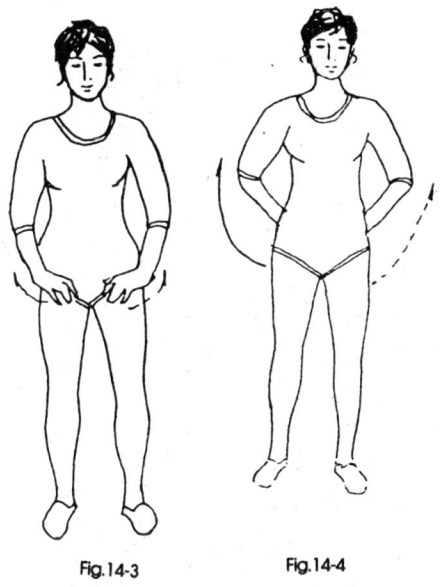

Fig. 14-3 Fig. 14-4

2. Curve around the anus and enter the kidneys at Mingmen (Figs. 14-3, 14-4).

The mind visualizes the Qi curving around the anus and reaching Changqiang. The hands move the Qi to the back. While inhaling move the hands upward to Mingmen. From there the Qi enters the kidneys. While breathing normally, tense the muscles of the abdomen, contract the muscles around the genitals and anus, and clench the teeth. Do this three times.

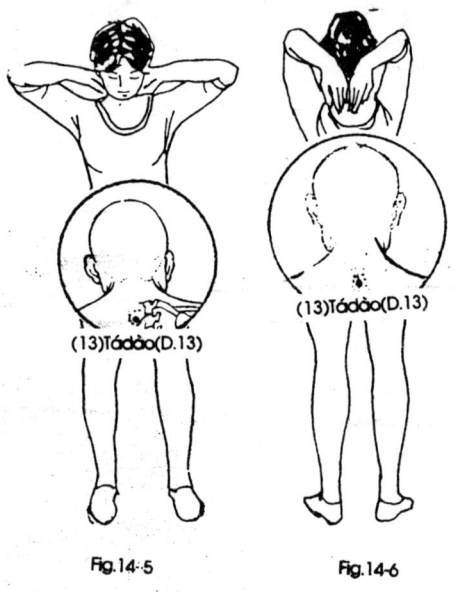

Fig.14-5   Fig.14-6

3. Stretch and raise the arms, move the Qi with the mind (Figs. 14-4, 14-5).

While inhaling move the hands upward along the route until the hands cannot go any higher. While exhaling drop the arms. While inhaling raise the arms over the head. At the same time, the mind moves the Qi upward along the route.

4. Drop the hands to touch Taodao and Dazhui (Fig. 14-5).

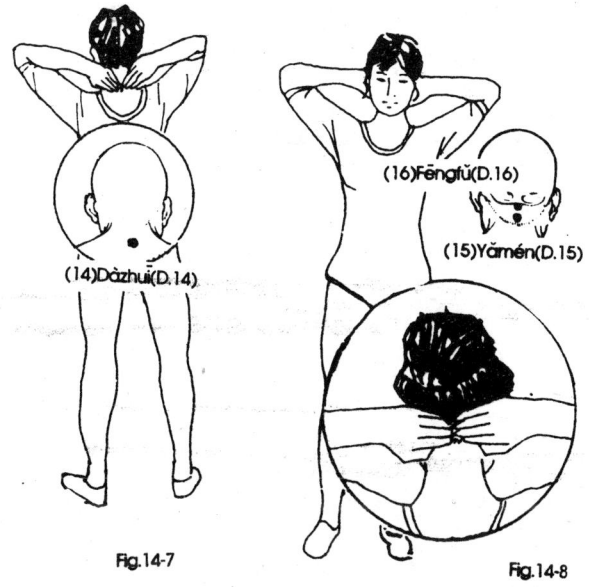

Fig.14-7   Fig.14-8

While exhaling drop the hands to touch Taodao (D. 13) and Dazhui (D. 14)

5. Ascend to Fengfu and enter the brain (Figs. 14-6, 14-7, 14-8).

While inhaling move the hands upward to the back of the neck. While breathing normally, put the middle fingers on Yamen (D. 15) and the ring fingers on Fengfu (D. 16). Massage the two points six times. Visualize the Qi entering the brain.

Fig. 14-9

6. Go to the vertex and press Baihui (Fig. 14-9).

While inhaling, move the hands to the vertex. While breathing normally, put the middle fingers on Baihui and press the point six times.

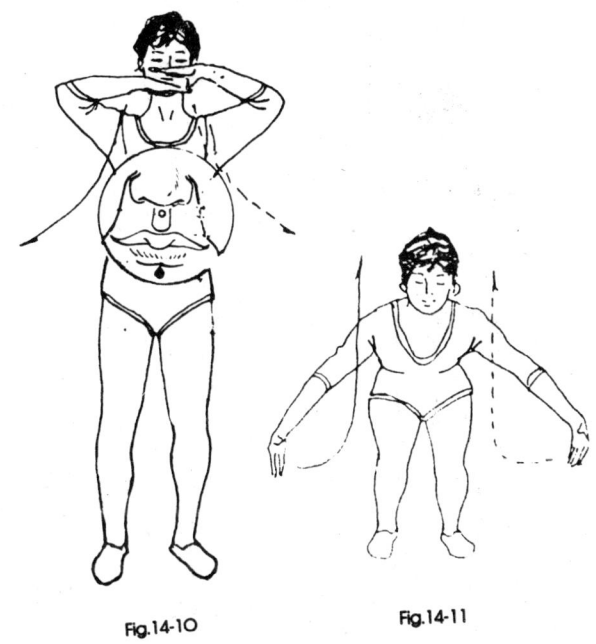

Fig.14-10 Fig.14-11

7. Massage the tips to link with the Ren Meridian (Fig. 14-10).

Move the hands along the route to the mouth. Massage above and below the lips back and forth six times. The Qi reaches Yinjiao. At that time, the Du Meridian is linked with the Ren Meridian. The Qi circulates through the Ren Meridian and the Du Meridian.

8. Bend the knees and hold the Qi (Fig. 14-11).

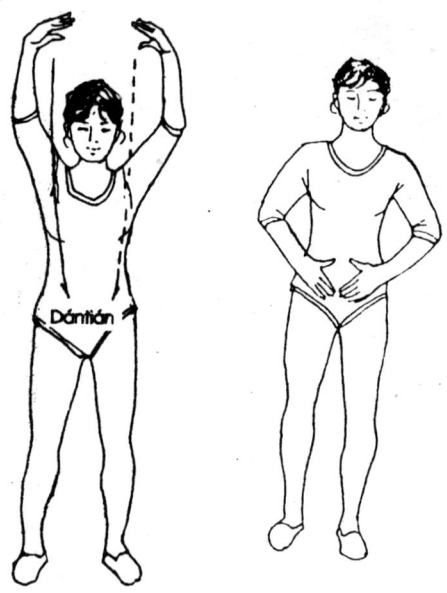

Fig. 14-13

9. Straighten the body and lift the arms over the head (Fig. 14-12).
10. Pour the Qi into Dantian (Fig. 14-12).
11. Concentrate on Dantian (Fig. 14-13).

The hands are on Dantian. Concentrate on Dantian for awhile. You should be in a state of stillness as you concentrate only on Dantian. Tense the abdomen, contract the muscles around the genitals and anus, and clench the teeth. Do this three times.

12. Ending form: lift the heels (Fig. 14-14).

Concentrate on Dantian. While inhaling deeply, lift the heels.

13. Ending form drop the heels (Figs. 14-15, 14-16).

While Exhale and drop the heels, while maintaining concentration on Dantian.

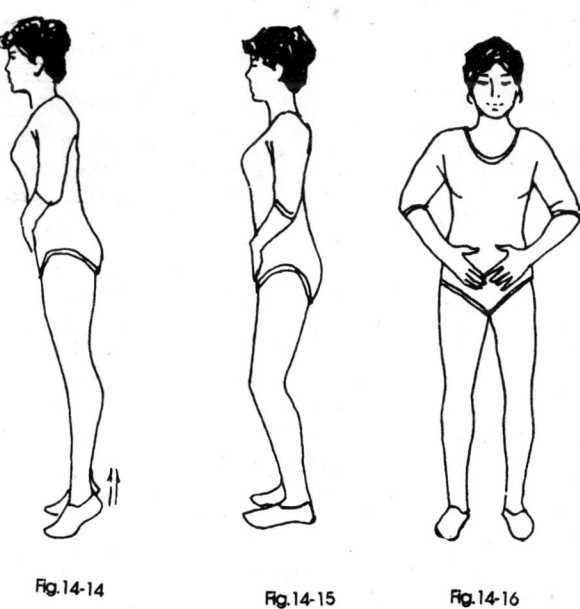

Fig. 14-14   Fig. 14-15   Fig. 14-16

14. Ending form return to the original posture (Fig. 14-17)

Continue to concentrate on Dantian for awhile. Then relax the whole body.

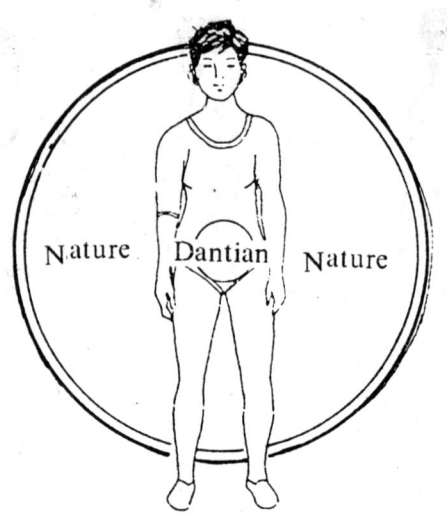

Fig. 14-17

Traditional Chinese Therapeutic Exercises and Techniques

Atlas of Therapeutic Motion for Treatment and Health
A Guide to Traditional Chinese Massage and Exercise Therapy

Traditional Chinese Therapeutic Exercises and Techniques
Standing Pole

Chinese Single Broadsword
A Primer of Basic Skills and Performance Routines for Practitioners

14-Series Sinew-Transforming Exercises

Infantile *Tuina* Therapy

Eating Your Way to Health
Dietotherapy in Traditional Chinese Medicine

Keep Fit the Chinese Way

Meridian Qingong

Taiji Qigong
Twenty-Eight Steps

经络气功

李丁 编著

李东 候敏 翻译

*

外文出版社出版

(中国北京百万庄路 24 号)

邮政编码 100037

北京外文印刷厂印刷

1988 年(34 开)第一版

1993 年第二次印刷

(英)

ISBN 7−119−00777−7 / R·18（外）

Distributed by
China International Book Trading Corporation
35 Chegongzhuang Xilu
Beijing 100044, China
P.U.Box 399, Beijing, China
00850   14-E-2378p